Tl

Keith Hill is a New Zealand writer and filmmaker. Born in Auckland in 1957, his early poetry was published in *Mate* and *Pilgrims*. During visits to India in 1979 and 1991 he worked on translations of the poetry of Mirabai and Kabir and *The Bhagavad Gita*. His novel, *Blue Kisses*, was published by HarperCollins NZ in 1998. He then turned to non-fiction, exploring the ways culture, history, religion, philosophy and mysticism have contributed to today's spiritual outlooks. During this period he wrote the Ashton Wylie Award winners *Striving To Be Human* (2007) and *The God Revolution* (2011), the latter applauded by Kirkus Review for discussing 'a wide range of academically abstruse subjects in consistently lucid, nontechnical prose.'

Keith has worked in the film and television industries since the early 1980s. He contributed to over fifty short films and music videos, with short films he produced premiering in international festivals and winning awards. His dramatic feature, *This is Not a Love Story* (2003), won Best Screenplay in the US indie festival DancesWithFilms and was a finalist in the 2004 NZ Film and TV Awards.

In 1991 Keith co-founded Rattle Records, working with leading New Zealand musicians, including Philip Dadson, Gitbox Rebellion, John Psathas, Dan Poynton, Gillian Whitehead, Michael Houstoun and taongo pouro masters Hirini Melbourne and Richard Nunns. From the early 2000s Keith documented recording sessions on video, publishing them on his YouTube channel, AttarMedia.

He continues to work across diverse media.

Interrogations

Selected writing 1976–1990

Keith Hill

First published in 2024 by Disjunct Books
an imprint of Attar Books, New Zealand

Paperback ISBN 978-1-0670143-0-8
Hardcover ISBN 978-1-0670143-1-5

Cover and interior design by Area Design
Cover photograph by Florian Klauer

Disjunct Books is published by Attar Books, a New Zealand
publisher that focuses on work that explores today's spiritual
experiences, culture, concepts and practices. For more information
visit Attar Books' website:

www.attarbooks.com
www.keithhillauthor.org

Contents

Interrogations ———— [2022]

Why are we concerned with art? To cross our frontiers, exceed our limitations, fill our emptiness – fulfil ourselves. This is not a condition but a process, in which what is dark in us slowly becomes transparent. In this struggle with one's own truth, the theatre has always seemed to me a place of provocation.

– Jerzy Grotowski

On Green Dolphin Street

The white-disced moon above a skyline of silhouetted rooftops illuminates the setting. The repetition of thoughts, of words, of tight smiles in confused rooms marks the time. Doubtless past ages have seen the same. Human chronicle is full of recycled dramas, recurring mistakes.

Here history observes a scarred street lit by the yellow circles of street lamps. A dog rounds the corner, cocks his leg, spurts, then trots away. Not history. Individuals arrive, make or do not make their mark, then vanish; human continuity remains. History, the record of this continuity, sees itself and shudders.

The street lamps remain impassive, waiting. Such a light stands here, on this corner. Time passes. The pupil expands.

From the doorway of an apartment building comes the clatter of hard-heeled shoes. A figure emerges and moves down the steps. As the figure passes under the street lamp starkness shows a young woman. She walks slowly through the light and on down the street. Then, just as she draws level with a line of rubbish bins, 'Damn!', she stumbles. She hops back to the street lamp and, leaning against it, slips off the offending shoe. One of its straps has broken. Mouth pursed, she stares down the street.

Above her, just one window open, the apartment building reaches four stories into the black night sky: a head ducks back from view and bang! the window closes. Startled, a cat leaps from behind the rubbish bins and streaks across the road, disappearing into the alley opposite.

From the apartment block comes the sound of a slow walk. A figure limps down the cracked steps. Hesitates. Then limps into the lamp light. The figure is a young woman. Her dress is ripped up one thigh. In the pale yellow light she inspects the broken shoe in her hand. Turns it over and over. Then she clasps it to her chest and takes a grimacing step out of the circle of light, into the street's darkness.

'Where has she come from? Where going?'

An acrid smell wafts from the rubbish bins. Somewhere close a toilet flushes, a man coughs. A young woman steps out of the darkness into the circle of light. Well dressed, face carefully made up, but shown streaked in the lamp-cast yellow. She stands there, silent. Tears in her eyes, the whole street reflected in them, upside-down.

'Where has she come from? Where – '

From out of a tangle of shadows a figure steps. A car screeches round the corner and spotlights parted lips, enormous eyes. For a moment. Then speeds past and vanishes from view.

Dishevelled, make-up smudged, she limps into the lamp light and slips off one shoe. Soleless. And the strap too has snapped. 'Where from? Going ... ?' A cat leaps from behind rubbish bins and streaks across the road. A window slams shut. Her eyes reflect the street upside-down.

Above her, above the street, above the skyline of silhouetted roofs, the white-disced moon observes. History too stands watching. Patient recorder, it perceives what is happening, without comment. Where the street light stands a yellow circle on the worn pavement and a limping shape recedes into the dark.

A Brief History of the World, Part 1 _____ [1984]

The Catalogue of an Ordinary Life

CHARACTERS

YOUNG MAN
YOUNG WOMAN
OLDER MAN
OLDER WOMAN
VOICE

The characters all look as if they have been woken up in the middle of the night and transported to where they are. YOUNG MAN has a cut on his forehead and is dishevelled, suggesting he has been in a fight. YOUNG WOMAN wears combined pyjamas and clothing. OLDER MAN is wearing pyjamas and a dressing gown. OLDER WOMAN wears an evening gown which is torn. Her make up is smeared.

SETTING

A basement. Several pieces of furniture are piled in one corner, notably two armchairs, a rolled square of carpet, a standard lamp, and a straight-backed chair. From high on the left wall, down the back wall, and ending just above the floor on the right wall, runs a large diameter metal tube. A pole sits in the middle of the stage, to the top of which is fixed a loudspeaker.

Know what is in your sight, and what is hidden will be revealed to you. – *The Gospel According to Thomas*

Darkness.

The sound of a harmonica.

Lights up.

YOUNG MAN is playing the harmonica.

OLDER MAN consults a pocket-watch.

OLDER WOMAN is filing her nails.

YOUNG WOMAN moans, wakes, raises her head, stands,
walks around groggily.

She approaches OLDER MAN, who continues examining
the watch.

She approaches OLDER WOMAN, who looks up, smiles
tightly, keeps filing.

She approaches YOUNG MAN, who ignores her and
plays the harmonica.

She knocks the harmonica from his mouth.

He stares at her.

She stares back.

Pause.

The loudspeaker crackles.

> LOUDSPEAKER
> Hello. Testing. One, two, three. Four, five,
> seven. Okay. Attention. Attention. Greetings
> mortals. This – uh – this is God speaking.

OLDER WOMAN kneels, then bows her head.

OLDER MAN considers, then does the same.

YOUNG MAN and YOUNG WOMAN turn towards the
loudspeaker, otherwise don't move.

LOUDSPEAKER

I have a message. Our sensors indicate doubt in this vicinity. Be assured. I am here. I will show myself presently. Meanwhile be kind to one another. I am the shepherd and you're my flock. Remember. Be happy. Be good. That is all.

The loudspeaker clicks off.
The two raise their heads.
YOUNG WOMAN looks at YOUNG MAN.
He walks away.
YOUNG WOMAN approaches OLDER MAN and OLDER WOMAN and examines them.
They look back at her.
Pause.
YOUNG MAN plays the harmonica.
OLDER MAN stands.
Goes to the corner.
Picks up the armchair.
Carries it towards the centre of the space, where he places it.
Gets the standard lamp.
Puts it beside the chair.
Goes through the pile of newspapers.
Selects one.
Returns to the armchair.
Turns on the lamp: it casts no light.
Sits.
Reads the newspaper.
Pause.
OLDER WOMAN walks to the OLDER MAN, looks at him.
Sits in his lap.
Puts her arms around him.
He puts an arm around her.
Pause.

YOUNG WOMAN approaches YOUNG MAN.

He stops playing.

They look at one another.

Silence.

Rattling, off.

An object rolls down the metal tube.

A box falls out onto the floor.

The four stare at it.

Pause.

YOUNG WOMAN approaches the box.

OLDER MAN and OLDER WOMAN stand.

Draw away from the box.

YOUNG WOMAN reaches into the box.

Hesitates.

Pulls out an apple.

Hesitates.

Bites into it.

Hesitates.

Chews.

Pause.

She takes a second bite, chews.

The three relax.

Approach the box.

Take out food.

Sit.

OLDER MAN, OLDER WOMAN and YOUNG WOMAN
eat hungrily.

YOUNG MAN stands away from them.

Screams, off.

The screams build in intensity.

OLDER WOMAN continues eating.

OLDER MAN pauses, listens briefly, then continues eating.

YOUNG MAN walks around, seeking the scream's direction.

YOUNG WOMAN lifts food to her mouth, tries to eat, can't.

The screams die.

OLDER MAN and OLDER WOMAN continue eating.

YOUNG WOMAN remains sitting.

YOUNG MAN plays the harmonica.

OLDER MAN and OLDER WOMAN finish eating.

Young man stops playing the harmonica.

Silence.

OLDER WOMAN stands.

Stretches.

Walks to the pile of discarded furniture.

Lies down behind a large box, only her feet visible.

OLDER MAN stands.

Walks over to the same place.

Looks down.

Lies down on OLDER WOMAN, only their entwined feet visible. They grunt, sigh.

The loudspeaker crackles.

OLDER MAN's face appears above the top of the furniture.

OLDER WOMAN's face appears beside it.

The loudspeaker continues to crackle.

OLDER WOMAN and OLDER MAN stand.

Fasten their clothing.

Walk to the pole.

They signal YOUNG WOMAN.

She looks at YOUNG MAN.

He looks away.

YOUNG WOMAN joins them.

The three kneel in front of the pole and bow their heads.

> LOUDSPEAKER
> Attention. Attention. I, God, have an announcement to – uh – announce. I will instruct you further on the practice of being good. Mortals smell. Not physically – I mean, yes, mortals

do smell physically – but what – uh – I am referring to, fundamentally, is the moral stench of all those engaged in human society. Hence I have decided on a remedy. All mortals, without exception, will make a confession. To me. This confession will lead to moral impurities being expunged from said mortal's soul. That – uh – that is the substance of my instructions. Remember. Be happy. Be good. That is all.

The loudspeaker is switched off.
The three stand.
Look at each other.
OLDER MAN approaches the pile of furniture.
Selects a chair.
Sets it facing and close to the loudspeaker.
Indicates OLDER WOMAN to sit on it.
She does.

OLDER WOMAN
I've never been so bad that I need to confess anything. Except I get annoyed sometimes. At the way things move around. Objects. People. Emotions. You just get used to the way things are, then something changes and you have to adjust all over again. It's frustrating. Life could be so simple. If it wasn't for the sinister rebellion of things. I wasn't happy when I first found myself here. Not remembering where I had been before. Not knowing how long I'll be staying. It's disturbing. But I adjusted. And now I can't imagine being anywhere else. God, believe me, please. I will obey you always. I am happy. I am good.

She stands, walks away.
OLDER MAN sits.

>OLDER MAN
>My confession is not easy to make. I've killed.
>Who? Not who. What. I've killed a thousand
>hopes and opportunities. If every opportunity is
>a planet, and each planet part of a solar system
>of possibilities, I've allowed a galaxy of potential
>experiences to pass me by. And an opportunity
>once passed never returns. So what have I left?
>Gnashing teeth? A sense of futility? Not at all.
>I've given our situation here a great deal of
>thought. And I've come to the conclusion there
>is no other world. Of course, there may be other
>rooms. Almost definitely there are other rooms.
>But another world – it's not possible. And why
>should there be? We don't need it. Besides, if we
>want to ask questions, that's not a question we
>should be asking. The real question is why are we
>here? The answer to which is obvious. We've been
>chosen. We're the elite which has been chosen
>and brought here for some purpose which as yet
>is known only to God, but which, in due course,
>he will, most certainly, reveal to us. Let me affirm:
>God, I am ready. I accept you. I believe! I thought
>I might be able to cry. But I can't.

He stands, walks away.
YOUNG WOMAN sits.

>YOUNG WOMAN
>I confess to the worst sin of all. I doubt God.
>I stare at my surroundings and wonder: Why?
>Why are we here? Why aren't we somewhere

else? Why is this life ... why isn't it better? I don't understand why we were put here, in a place we were never consulted about, by someone whose presence is undeniable, but whose motives I can't help but suspect. I – I want to believe. But ... I doubt. I doubt myself. I doubt my ability to carry out God's instructions. I doubt I'm worthy of God's love and concern. Because I want to play my part in what's happening. Whatever that is. I do. I want – I want to be wanted. Just show me how to act. Please. I'll be good. I'll carry it out. And I'll try to be happy. I promise.

She stands and walks away.
The three look at YOUNG MAN.
He doesn't move.
OLDER WOMAN indicates the chair.
YOUNG MAN doesn't move.
OLDER MAN moves towards YOUNG MAN.
Halts in front of him.
Pause.
YOUNG MAN approaches the chair.
Hesitates.
Stands on the chair.
Raises his hands to his mouth.
Hold.

      YOUNG MAN
      Fuck God!

Pause.
OLDER MAN and OLDER WOMAN approach the YOUNG MAN.
Pull him off the chair.
Drag him to the pole.

While OLDER WOMAN holds him, OLDER MAN takes
the cord off his dressing gown.
He ties YOUNG MAN's hands behind him, around the
pole.
OLDER MAN and OLDER WOMAN return to chair.
Sit.
YOUNG WOMAN approaches YOUNG MAN, stares at
him.
The loudspeaker crackles.
The three approach loudspeaker, kneel and bow their heads.

> LOUDSPEAKER
> Attention. Attention. Your souls are beginning
> to sparkle. We – that is, uh, I – have decided
> that, because of your obedience to – my –
> instructions, you have earned a reward. Please
> stand by to take delivery of your reward.
> Remember. All good things come to those who
> wait. You are all equal in my eyes. Be happy. Be
> good. That is all.

The loudspeaker clicks off.
OLDER MAN and OLDER WOMAN stand.
Rattling, off.
An object rolls down the metal tube.
A box falls out onto the floor.
The three stare at it. YOUNG MAN stares out at the
audience.
Silence.
YOUNG WOMAN moves to the box.
Opens it.
Takes out a television.
OLDER MAN and OLDER WOMAN take it from her, set it
up with the screen facing away from the audience, plug it
in.

OLDER WOMAN selects a chair.

Sits in front of the television.

OLDER MAN places a chair beside hers, sits.

YOUNG WOMAN watches them.

Glances towards YOUNG MAN.

Pause.

YOUNG WOMAN selects a chair from the pile of
furniture.

Places it beside the two.

Approaches the television.

Turns up the sound: static is heard.

Returns to chair.

Sits.

Static sound continues.

The three watch.

OLDER WOMAN glances at OLDER MAN.

She puts her hand on his knee.

Strokes his thigh.

Without taking his eyes off the television, OLDER MAN
reaches down, moves her hand, puts it into his lap,
continues watching the television.

The three watch.

Pause.

> YOUNG WOMAN
> No!

> OLDER WOMAN
> Ssshhhh!

> OLDER MAN
> Be happy.

> OLDER WOMAN
> Be good.

YOUNG WOMAN stands, approaches YOUNG MAN.
Unties his hands.
OLDER MAN and OLDER WOMAN stand, turn, and face
YOUNG WOMAN.

> OLDER MAN
> What are you doing?

> YOUNG WOMAN
> God said be happy. This doesn't make me happy.

> OLDER MAN
> But he isn't good.

> YOUNG WOMAN
> Does tying him up make him good? Look at him.
> He's unhappy.

> OLDER MAN
> If we make him happy we make God unhappy.
> And if God isn't happy that isn't good.

> YOUNG WOMAN
> But making the world a good place makes
> everyone happy.

> OLDER WOMAN
> Whatever makes me happy is good enough for
> me.

OLDER WOMAN turns, sits in her chair.
YOUNG WOMAN finishes untying YOUNG MAN.
OLDER MAN turns, sits in his chair.
YOUNG WOMAN looks at YOUNG MAN.
He looks back at her.
Pause.
The loudspeaker crackles.

The two stand, approach the loudspeaker, kneel.
YOUNG WOMAN starts to turn, YOUNG MAN holds her.
They look at each other.
YOUNG WOMAN pulls away, approaches the loudspeaker,
kneels and bows her head.

> LOUDSPEAKER
> Attention. Attention. I, God, am satisfied – with
> – satisfied with – satisfied with – (thump) – I,
> God, am satisfied with the progress being made.
> Three cheers. Well done. For everything there
> is a season. You can make a silk purse out of a
> sow's ear. We – uh – I – will provide you with
> the materials you need to make the world a
> better place in which to live. Everything –

The loudspeaker dies, because YOUNG MAN has moved
the chair, stood in it, and ripped out the loudspeaker's
wires.
The three raise their heads.
Stand.
Look.
YOUNG MAN walks away.
OLDER MAN follows him.
OLDER WOMAN climbs the chair, tries to reconnect the
wires.
OLDER MAN grabs YOUNG MAN by his shirt.
Pause.
The speaker crackles.
OLDER MAN releases younger man and steps back.
The loudspeaker crackles and pops, but no voice is heard.
The loudspeaker gives a final BURP! and falls silent.

> OLDER WOMAN
> For everything there is a season.

OLDER MAN
You can make a silk purse out of a sow's ear.

OLDER WOMAN
Remember.

OLDER MAN
Be happy.

OLDER WOMAN
Be good.

OLDER MAN and OLDER WOMAN approach the
television.
Sit in their chairs.
Watch.
Pause.
YOUNG MAN moves towards YOUNG WOMAN.
She steps away.
She joins the two.

OLDER MAN
A stitch in time saves nine.

OLDER WOMAN
Every cloud has a silver lining.

OLDER WOMAN
Remember.

OLDER MAN
Be happy.

OLDER WOMAN
Be good.

OLDER MAN
That is all.

YOUNG WOMAN sits.

The three watch television.

Static is heard.

Screams, off.

Continue.

Die.

The static sound fades.

Silence.

YOUNGER MAN plays a tune on the harmonica.

A thump, off.

YOUNG MAN stops playing.

A door opens at the rear of the stage. Lights pours
through.

YOUNG MAN walks to the door.

Looks.

He walks back to the three.

They don't move.

>YOUNG MAN
>Wake up!

No response.

He shakes the YOUNG WOMAN.

No response.

He walks back to the door.

Halts.

Looks at the others.

Turns, faces the light.

Hesitates.

Walks through.

Disappears.

Pause.

The YOUNG WOMAN raises her head.

Stands.

Looks towards the door.

Takes a step towards it.

Pause.

Steps back.

Pause.

The door closes.

Silence.

YOUNG WOMAN approaches the door.

She tries to open it: there is no handle.

She hammers on it.

Halts.

Pause.

The loudspeaker crackles.

Pops.

Stops crackling.

>YOUNG WOMAN
>God?

YOUNG WOMAN approaches the pole.

Looks up at the loudspeaker.

>YOUNG WOMAN
>God? Speak to me. Guide me. Comfort me. I want
>to believe. I try to follow your instructions. But it's
>so difficult. I wait your call.

Silence.

>YOUNG WOMAN
>God?

She shakes the pole.

>YOUNG WOMAN:
>Can you hear me, God?

She sinks onto the floor.
The lights begin to fade.
YOUNG WOMAN starts to sob.

>YOUNG WOMAN
>God?

Pause.

>YOUNG WOMAN
>G-o-d?

Her sobs die.
Silence.
Slow fade to black.

Waymarks ____ [1976–1977]

Time (for a change)

Sunrise over the empty lots.
She walks the dim part of this soiled city,
the slow streets and fog drifting,
down to where the wrecks lay beached and wane,
& while she hears the shells crush beneath her feet,
numbing her desires, these thoughts,
her veins burn,
& waves lap through the mist.

She walks this rippled sand,
where waves wash the steps she takes again,
heart docked in this mortal wharf,
& she thinks of that ebbing past, forever gone,
how maybe, re-created in some future time ...
but past & present are just her desiring thoughts
& time will prove their change
as she moves through mist
that shrouds her life from what is real:
this present eternity fired in silence ...

Desire flows through her veins,
but hope does too,
& the vision of a few strong sunflowers
lifting through the sand
seeking eternity beyond time's fog,
& so she feels the sun above the haze of her life
& the heart burning in her blood saying:
It's time for a change.

The Choice

Between sun's flame & pale earth we ride,
a spirited animal graven in our frail machine,
& we're blindly through this city
with its greasy streets that smear our trafficked life,
shedding water, to leave our aspiring spirit low & dry.
But it's here, overrun by desolation,
that hope is unearthed,
for these sorry streets haunted
by animal passions changing
illuminate in their darkness
the unwavering sun high above this inconstant city.

From the wombed sea humanity came,
when earth met light,
our spirits from deep space
many times returning to this choice planet,
seeking that peace-filled life beyond birth & death.
But this city's landed us lost in separation,
where unconscious, automatically impassioned,
desires turn us off & on,
& we're dead to the choice of free-willing souls.

Humanity of darkest earth! The stars in sadness
weep their light onto your dessicated hearts,
freeing your will for the primal choice:
this mechanical city or the bright spirit aspiring –
they hear your cries echoing in these empty streets.
Unconscious humanity & suffering,
let mechanical death die
& turn your earthbound desire to the sun!

Tapestry

Within the scope & colour of her being
she's sharp needled by humanity's blue
of letting blunt ignorance loom.
Tired of fabrications
she wants to find what pattern it really is
her thread of being weaves in the cosmic tapestry.

Tied in this knot, she sees all experience
rainbows here, on life's vast cloth,
coloured black through purest white.
So too she's a thread in hue all hues, just disarrayed,
knotted now but one day loosed,
for life's mystery looms her round
but she too is that pattern, a trace in the cosmic weave,
so to know herself is to see the tapestry in itself
& become a being white containing all colours.

As above, so below, the pattern's wove right through,
& she's tangled but unravelling,
a knife for knowing she must clear her colour & pattern
& become a being disappeared into life's pure tapestry.

Billabong

Sun's disc & flaming.
Beneath, the desert's a swelter of undulating death,
a waver haze of sand where no water's hugged
& a tiny figure plod plods through the dunes.

It trudges weary this haggard,
a lone girl wretched in the wilderness
whose thirsting eyes lament this world of baning waste
that drought her far from his all-watering lips.

Waved harsh with heat, she's sobbing across the bleak
when from the haze a sprout of trees & water
lavishes her eyes, whispering:
'His lips are barren, drink here while you can.'

World of crazed illusion that's becoming but never is!
She faces up into the burning sky
and feels the sun flame through her with a shiver:
the billabong's mirage!

So now, beneath the sun incinerate, it's on she lopes,
clothes arid & flaking naked,
her illusioned self raw-ravaged
yet her heart flaming for his soulful kiss.

Unseen on high, in a halo of clouds,
love lets drop a curtain of light rain falling.

Of the Fishing for Men

Greater than ever life's death, love's breath. Greater than ever small taste, the quenching of hunger.

Light's nets drag the pale shore. Fishing with longing, long fish of despair. Thrusting this spear that shatters pale life in a sea-tide of blood. Blood that's caught in the twining light's net. And this is the drowning sea's motion: wash and avast, up gasping and down. But better than ever life's death, love's breath.

He squirms in the net and his heart is speared. Spared from drowning by the ecstasy of knowing his hunger is feeding. For his heart is filled with the fishes of love and air. Fishes of near. Near and ever nearer to the caster of the spear.

Greater than ever life took, love's hook. And the dying from life into light is the lure.

Arrow Flighting

The duck of our days wings time's skies; an arrow's shot and it falls. Cries on the face of the waters, in the shuddering reeds.

Lamenting a wasted life's loss, the wakeful pluck the reeds of readiness from where still earth meets the swelling water's lap, and with the sharp knife of struggle fashions perfection's bow. They string this bow with knowledge. Then gathers the feathers of struggle and glues them with conscience to their straightened self. Thereafter they place himself in the hands of the shooter, who sharpens them to one-pointedness and tests them for strength. Finally, they are notched in the bow and shot into the skies.

And this is the quest: each one's life is an arrow, flighting for the mark of knowing. What wonder if it miss!

One for the Drunkards

The lovers' great thirstings revealed to them the cellars.
And the cellars were many days calling. But it was only
the lovers' dry lips that led them to hear.

    The deaf man is dry, from dryness he's deaf, and
talks to himself as he plunders the grape. But lovers
have wine, in ecstasy are drunk, so don't see the point in
skinning the other. For the wine existed before the grape
was conceived.

    The grape was mutated that the wine may be known.
Like a grape is each heart, and why it's on-trodden is
that wine may start flowing. The lover seeks those who
have chosen it so. For wine is the giving of the ecstasy of
knowing.

    The lover has wine, the grape-groper is trodden.
Life is the means, and each discovers his end.

The Passionate Pilgrim  [1977 – 1978]

1

Love, your vast bells toll my languished tale
That, empty else of a passionate heart,
Is filled with the sad and lingering wail
That tells of two, from one, too far apart.
From your bosomed belfry, you souling peal
The body's outer to strike inward, mine,
An awe-swelled spirit where resounds, so real,
The music of this longing-burdened chime.
Far-quarried song of lone life's emptiness,
It's your soft magic tolls how love conspires
To union, that the more I seek, the less
This far is liked, the nearer I aspire.
    So chime bells, of two to be wed as one,
      That these deep words prove not an empty son.

2

What a season it is, when the low moon
Bales its yellow face in melting madness
Across the fields, palely feigning to noon,
But falling on the stubble in sadness.
What a season's breathing, when the bared trees
Are ravaged by night, suffering that cruel wind
Which, though the scourge of all this world, none sees
But pilgrims seeking to salve what they've sinned.
Love, this season's mine: so many days I've
Sown wild weeds to your pure grace, but now weep,
A pale moon through the trees barely alive,
Sheafing this cold crop of sorrow I reap.
    You are the sun who lights up my sick moon,
      So help me birth a son from this, earth's womb.

3

When I observe a muscle of trout make
Its threshing silvered sprint against the swift
River, fighting to reach that peaceful lake
From which it was, love-spawned, first cast adrift;
When its sunned skin I see burn in quick fire
As it strives through the earthed waters to some
Nearer pool, leaping rocked rapids higher
And higher through desire to return home;
When this passionate pilgrim giving its
All in furious struggle wholly fills
My sight, I am emptied of other fits
And wishes, and desire for you me wills.
    This image is a bait on which I feed,
    By which the more you lure, the more I'm freed.

4

One Being, source of the whole cosmos, who
Only need say 'Be' and it is, nothing
Exists save you: from one boundlessness to
The other, from the least atom whirling
Within an atom's atom, to the prime
Galaxies you cause to light-speed it through
The mind-tripping immense of space and time –
All this vast pleroma moving in two
Magnitudes through the six directions – none
Of it is other than so many flecks
Of dust whirling in your cupped hands, your One
In fact hidden by these multiple specks.
    When the deep truth of this I dimly see,
    What else can I write but: your glory Be!

5

Meaning full, life leaps phenomenally
At my senses, birthing a rave of thoughts
Explaining, and hence meaning's high tally,
Yet all life's numbers derive from one source.
For while attached to my senses I'm lost,
In blindness struggling with the all's meanings,
Whereas to perceive truly, undream-tossed,
Any part of the all's numbered seemings,
Requires knowledge of that One which all is
Derived from, sustained by, there returning;
Hence I separate from my senses this
Truth confounds, likewise from false discerning.
    Only through neglecting the six and the five
    Is One found: by thus departing, we arrive!

6

Under divine eyes that touch all with their
Loving gaze, I look at this view-filled life
But, blind to your sight, see only despair
And longing, twin blades of a single strife,
For this gift-confounding present stabs me
Deep through with separation's sad heartache,
But it's not your absence from what I see
Which thus wounds, causing this sharp pain to wake,
Rather (for being presence itself you
Are always here) it derives from me not
Knowing where my true eyes lie, for the view
Seen depends on the viewer, and thus what
    I am lacking is not the sight to see,
    But knowledge of my own reality.

7

Through the Garden of Eden (this world) Eve
And Adam walked lost in sensual pleasure,
Asleep and unknowing, when from the tree
Uncoiled love's snake, offering choice's treasure.
For tasting that apple they awoke to
Good and evil (wisdom and ignorance)
And how lack gripped them: suddenly, they knew
They were denuded of spiritual grace.
Thus have we been left to clothe ourselves with
Knowledge, to confront the gaping abyss
That keeps us from ourselves, to climb the cliff
Of knowing as we ascend towards bliss.
    O blessed day when that apple was bit
    And I saw this Eden had to be quit!

8

Sin does not exist, save in those low states
Of ignorance that lead fools to noise it;
Good has no existence save what gates
The truth-seeker into states beyond it.
Only wisdom and ignorance: but what
Takes one higher lowers another, so
To each his own, left in peace, for there's not
Many know enough to say, truth-filled, no.
More than one path to wisdom and each must
Needs discover his own way of walking;
More than one way to know you and bust
Senseless ignorance with all its baulking.
    Philosophy should both unite and divide:
    Teach us to walk with both eyes open wide!

The dream that is the ego is the curse
Of those who are seeking reality;
It's the sly Cain who would murderous immerse
The spirit's Abel in death, devilry
Incarnate whose sole aim is to banish
The self from a chance of earning a soul
And a taste of wisdom, to vanish
From sight that blissful state which is the goal.
It sees nothing of knowledge, peace or love;
It knows of nothing but itself, yet its
Self is farthest from it, while all above
It loves to hate, till it tears peace to bits.
    This is true and never proved a fable,
    Yet watch hearers change their names to Abel.

10   (After Rumi)

Not in any church, in any doctrine
Or creed, have I found your presence ever;
Though I've drunk the delightful wine
Of book upon book, they showed you never.
Among thousands of heads bobbing city
Streets I found not even a trace of Here;
I looked through nature, but though she's lovely
Form's another barrier: you weren't there.
And so I searched all this world's coloured wealth,
I searched but in no place found your pure hue;
Till at last I was left with but myself,
When yes! deep in my own heart, there was you.
    How strange that though from you we are so far,
    You're closer to us than our jugular!

11

Ah, this so-called wonderful state named life
Is nothing, just so many daggers hung
On time's necklace and stretched in bleeding strife
From womb to tomb, causing all who are flung
Upon it to suffer that pain which lives
On its blades and is dealt them who, seeking
Pleasure, become attached to what it gives:
For always it dies and leaves them weeping.
So what then have this life and I to do
With each other? My one beloved, I
Would become non-attached to all but you
And, in this world not of it, to it, die.
    True one, bring to this lowly life your love
    That, seeking more, I may find you above.

12

Minute among the smooth-worn driftwood
Thrown up by the storm, I'm but a speck of sand
Lost on this world's shore, under its volcano,
Feeling myself in some strange borderland.
For all here is tainted by the bitter
Ash taste of mortality: the seagull's
Wheeling flight, the beach writhing in winter,
None escapes what emptied these wave-lapped shells.
Just so the toothed wind howls for my quick death,
Would snatch me seawards to navigate
The unknown's waves, ride destruction's cold breath,
Till what I am death wholly obliterates.
    Only this hope remains if we would still be:
    A built soul-boat, transporting us to eternity.

13

In the sweet, honeyed days of summer's sighs,
When wandering scents blossom across the sea,
High on mystery's winds a bird freely flies,
At the flower's full lips, there sucks a bee.
Look! Is that sunlight shatters a dewdrop,
Flowering a cool rainbow where once none fell?
And can you hear how the wind's whispers stop,
To sound still in an empty sea-kissed shell?
For though the waves ebb and flow, it's tranquil,
While from its depths a many-hued bird rears;
The whole sighing world its eye seems to fill:
Flamed by the sun, at last it disappears.
    If all this dreamed world breathes such mystery,
    How much more so, then, love's reality?

14

Sun's shafts cut the night, waken the flowers,
Laughing to light the twigs glistening below;
Webbed, a spider's stranded, shakes dew showers:
Hanging, circling, it has nowhere to go.
Yet now shrugs a drop, escaping the web;
Now urges a trickle, knobbling down bark:
Down drooping hillsides, streams swelling the steppe,
This drop laps the bank from that wooded dark.
Until one joyful day the sea is glimpsed,
Its depths and waves where the sun's sparklings course;
Returning in love the drop homeward limps,
To vanish completely, drowned in its source.
    This is my longing, for this death I live;
    Till I reach my end, I'm love's fugitive.

Records of a Non-Plussed Being _____ [1978]

Peeling Posters

This small shaky wall
    offers the only respite
        from the moaning wind.

    Doll floating in the fountain,
    your stitched smile has come apart.

From the highest tree
    falls a soft shower of leaves,
        every one withered.

    Watching the jumping children,
    an old man forgets his pipe.

Large billowing clouds
    that fill the vastness of sky,
        dreams too fade away.

    Tired of this saddening world,
    the hotel man eyes his pills.

When the siren fades,
    and the bars all fall empty,
        the streetsweeper works.

    Posters peeling from the walls –
    perhaps this too is a dream.

Golden Years

Seven o'clock.
    The alarm rings to wake her
        lain stiff between cold sheets.

Kids hungry and toast burning –
Who has hidden the honey?

Husband pecks her cheek goodbye,
    leaves the house to clean,
        kids hungry again.

Trapped soul, what are your thoughts when –
Have to buy more toilet paper.

Dinner down their throats,
    dishes in the sink,
        they watch exciting TV.

Kids in bed and out gunning
he shoots into a cold tomb.

Rough snores beside her
    she listens to the rained streets,
        then closes her eyes.

Whatever her dreams this night,
the alarm will ring tomorrow.

The Silent

Children are running,
　　yelling and shouting through the streets
　　　　outside the house.

　　Telephone rings all day long,
　　but no one to answer it.

Twelve dry blades of grass
　　round a grave, while a lone hand
　　　　pushes up from underneath.

　　Rose fallen from the bride's bouquet,
　　trampled by the guest's black feet.

In Tel Aviv, Dublin,
　　politicians toast speeches –
　　　　the guns are talking.

　　Children's book about heroes,
　　its pages clotted with blood.

In a dark labyrinth
　　of earth, the cramped seed toils:
　　　　why doesn't it sprout?

　　Tears running, an old woman
　　at the window mouths voicelessly.

Love Story

In the city of bland streets
the billboards drip with colour.

Across the casino
Bill drunkenly leers at bored women:
Life's a gamble ... or ... ?

*

Eyes hot with tears,
     she stares from the high window
         at a street of blurred neon.

Trembling curtain held
     in her hand ... what design stands
         in the faded pattern?

*

With a single heave
Bill vomits into the alley,
retrieves his false teeth.

     Hotel window above,
     the curtain gracefully drops.

Heavy traffic, man!
Yet from a speeding taxi falls
the hint of a destination.

*

Trailing her scarf
    the actress rejoins her friends,
        their palms extended.

    False hopes and true prophecies:
    the fortune-teller counts the sighs.

In the next room plays
    a record of the latest sou ...
        latest sou – lates –

*

    Sc-r-r-e-e-u-n-ch!

*

His head on fire,
Bill staggers, drops, stands, staggers,
clatters among the cans.

Their fingers nimble, the boys
empty every loaded pocket.

*

In a slow flowing
    wash of red, wine spreads across
        the white tablecloth.

    Cursing the 'Bloody world!', she
    threatens, 'Right now!' to 'Do something!'

Taking no notice,
    the party guests turn away,
        conversing in LOW TONES.

*

A door slams in the night,
heels clatter a sharp tattoo.

    Swearing furiously,
    she runs down the dark alley,
    falls over (poor) Bill.

A swift kick in the gut,
one shoe remains in his shirt.

    Moist eyes, shapely legs,
    an elegant limp – what more
    does a lady need?

Thud! The sports car door closes,
red tail lights merge with the night.

* *
* BENEATH THE STRIP-TEASE NEON *
* *

    Bill climbs to his feet, s

              ta

        gg

              e

          sr
    weaves off into the shadows.

Dry squeak repeating,
the LOVE TUB sign swings to
             and
         fro.

Salad Days

Signing papers, the manager
waits lunchtime recreation.

From a window next door,
onto the pavement below,
a boy drops marbles.

In the mahogony office
his mother drops names.

*

In the concrete square,
    office workers on a break
        rail against the wind.

Stock downturns, dark depressions:
who controls what goes where?

A splash of olive oil
    garnishes a perfect green salad:
        LOOK AT THAT SHARE PRICE!

In the velvet-lined back room
the bankers are out to lunch.

*

Crusts dry and curled ...
    the temp ignores the sandwich
        and goes for a Caesar.

How much bigger can it get?
IT'S THE SALE OF THE CENTURY!

In a mad flurry
    starving shoppers flood the aisles
      devouring bargains.

In the street outside marbles
bounce high between parked cars.

        *

Payslips finally signed off,
the manager turns his train set ON.

Out of the tunnel,
the manager's train goes round and
round, round and round,
      round and r
          o
          u
          u
          n
          d . . . .

The Lighthouse

Children's sandcastle ...
    the cold waves wash and you melt
      back into the sea.

      From the over-waves unknown
  a distant wind comes whispering.

Through the worn wharf's piles,
    as it shifts the sand in streams,
      the wind is singing.

*

Large summer raindrops
splatter the road's hot tarseal –
moist tangy smell rises.

      From a car full of drunk boys
  a beer bottle comes flying.

Stumbling across love
she is laid on her back,
sky of stars shooting.

*

On the wave-bashed rocks,
    beneath the looming lighthouse,
      each oyster is tight shut.

      Old fisherman, rod in hand,
  what is the meaning of it all?

As storm clouds gather,
    and the gulls screech, the fisherman
        spits into the sea.

*

In church happy families hug:
the flash cameras snap.

    Under a red-skied dusk
    a new-born baby cries:
    marriage ring vindicated.

Dark rings under washed-out eyes,
paused at the window she sees ...

    Beyond the tyre-marked road,
    above the barnacled wharf,
    the huge lighthouse rears.

Bus Stop

Each in their own car,
    they drive back from work to their
        house in the suburbs.

Letter on the kitchen bench
quoting mortgage repayments.

    Limosined banker,
    you dine in fat restaurants –
    where does it come from?

In a dry fly-blown village
they clutch their starved babies.

Cold in the cafe,
    a man stares at his coffee,
        hungry for sugar.

Sniffing around the back door,
a dog finds only garbage.

    BUY NOW! PAY LATER!
    No society has ever made
    SO many SO happy.

Standing in the bus stop queue
he watches the packed bus speed past.

Departure Song

Grey smoke of incense
winding a crooked trail
into the night sky.
With two teary red-rimmed eyes,
her hurt heart burns in longing.

> What do you sing weeping girl,
> hair stuck to your face, lips blue?

'Take me home, my lord.
I am trapped on a slow train
going nowhere and
my one suitcase is empty.
Take me back home I pray.'

> Who hears your voice weeping girl,
> lost behind this blind life has drawn?

'Kiss this soul, my lord.
I am a clear pool into
which life throws pebbles,
and with each ripple I drown.
Save me from this I pray.'

> On the bridge above the black waters,
> a lone set of headlights moving.

Records of a Non-plussed Being

Being alive is a mysterious experience. This is a thought that could come to a sleepy observer, paused early one morning under the branches of a weather-battered pine to watch a flock of geese straggle across a dawn-stained sky.

I had woken with an overwhelming feeling that the road was calling me. So I packed my bag and hung a poem in the room.

> The straining white kite
> breaks its red anchoring line.
> Another rock floating free?

Walking along the road I could see the dark silhouette of the Ocean Beach freezing works across the harbour. I considered how sheep were prodded up to the slaughtermen waiting on the blood-stained platform.

> Above the lush pastures
> where the sheep graze by fence posts
> a swift kea glides.

Later, I stood listening to the waves lapping the sand and let my eyes linger on the handful of houses snuggled between the harbour and hill. For a moment I doubted the wisdom of leaving.

> Brown sparrows bathing
> in hollows of dirt – your dust
> gets into my eyes.

But a time always arrives when it is time to move on.

This road so unknown:
how many have walked where I
now wear out my shoes?

A sheep transporter dropped me off at a hostel. Before going to bed I spent a long time watching the sky.

How lucky I am,
the stars are above my head,
no hole in my shoe.

But the following morning, as I sat in the bus looking at the fields speeding past, this felt much too simplistic, because there remained a hole in my heart.

Small ant struggling
among the giant tree roots,
and below ... the void.

But Wanaka was so lovely it couldn't be ignored. There was no wind and the lake was a vast mirror reflecting the grey sky. Leaf-bare poplars stood on its perimeter, while far away loomed the snow-capped mountains. Yet, while the landscape truly was entrancing, my inner ache remained.

In the storm's centre
is there really such a place
as stillness and peace?

Later in the day a salesman gave me a ride. From the car we had an expansive view of Haast Pass. The flat valley floor, with mountains on either side, was framed by a rainbow which stretched over several peaks. Soon the road passed through an ancient beech forest. The trees were beautiful in their creeper-hung dankness, and the thought that they had been there for thousands of years was awe-inspiring. However, after this magnificent build-up, Haast was a surprise.

> O Haast, I thought you
> a large and bustling town ...
> well, well, well!

The salesman had business to attend to before continuing north. While waiting I went for a walk. Fifty shacks strung out alongside the railway track. Now old and ramshackle, they must once have been filled with workers' dreams and hopes, illusions and disillusions.

> Rails disappearing –
> my train too is wheeling
> through eternity.

Soon we were headed for Franz Joseph Glacier. I thanked the salesman and got out. Fortunately I was in time to purchase a guided tour up the rocky track to the glacier. Ten of us admired the glacier. From its foot cataracted a foaming rush of water. It was eerie to consider that for hundreds of thousands of years this glacier had been advancing and retreating up and down its scoured valley.

> Blue-white sloping tongue,
> you lap from huge mountain walls –
> we stand like ice grains.

Late that afternoon I hitched to Greymouth and stayed in a back-packers'. In the evening I wandered along an old wharf. The cold sea frothed and sucked at its tiers, while in the sky a full moon contended with the clouds. The wind chilled to the bone.

Great unwinking moon
broken on the cold waters ...
my heart too, impure.

Next day I caught two buses, and after seven hours of travel was in Onekaka. Onekaka stands on a large sweeping bay, cut off from the rest of the province by a high, sharp hill, on top of which are numbers of grey, smoothly-rounded boulders. Their presence so high up is bizarre. Onekaka itself, while very pretty, had an unsettling atmosphere.

This impression was reinforced by a local resident who described how one day she had been sleeping on the beach when she was woken by numerous women and children screaming and crying. But on standing she could see no-one.

Years later she learnt there had once been a Māori pa in the area. In those days of inter-tribal battles, the defenders decided to put their women and children into a cave and wall it up for their safety, intending to return and release them after the battle was over. Unfortunately, all the defenders were massacred. Local legend says that the cries of the imprisoned can still be heard.

My friends had problems with possums, which clomped across the roof each night, but were smart enough to avoid the traps laid for them.

Secrets? What secrets?
Sly-eyed dawn taps the window,
the trap still unsprung.

Soon it was time to leave. As the bus sped down the Takaka hill and onto flat countryside again, flying past bare fields waiting the touch of spring, I thought of the women and children walled up in the cave, and what their feelings must have been as they came to realise that no one would return to release them. Meditating on this, the wind-belted, wave-bashed ferry journey across Cook Strait did nothing to alter my mood. That night I stayed in the Wellington YMCA. The storm followed me into the city, rattling the windows all night.

> Night shivers once more,
> a stray cat paused to watch.
> What is there, my friend?

Early the following morning, before the city was fully awake, I was on the roadside, thumbing a ride. The weather was numbingly cold. But the road was slow, and by six that evening I had travelled only as far as Taihape. Tired and cold, I longed for a hot shower and a soft bed, but had to be satisfied with a mattress of pine needles, deep in a clump of tattered pines.

> Mysterious moon,
> sombre branches shrug the earth
> reaching up for you.

Fortunately, the next morning delivered a ride, and I was soon seated in the front seat of a low-slung sports car, making swift time up the Desert Road. We swept past desolate tussock countryside spotted with patches of frost, snow-capped Ruapehu towering over her two sister peaks.

> Forget strategies,
> get a firm hold on your hat,
> we are on the way!

My driver didn't talk. Instead, when I made a comment, he just laughed. Was he crazy? Maybe. The road unrolling behind us, I fell into a reverie.

> With a touch of madness
> in us, that is poetry,
> we streak this road.

We hit Cambridge in time for lunch. Ned, my driver, went in search of a burger, leaving me on a bench in a park, eating a roll. A misty rain started to fall. Not far away was a small grove of trees. Under them sat a young woman who had opened up her shirt and was suckling her baby.

I was close enough to see she was crying. My heart went out to her. Or maybe that wasn't quite what happened there. Maybe it was me who wanted a comforting arm put around his shoulder?

Right then Ned pulled up, full of go. I watched the woman seated beneath the tree, rocking her baby, until she had vanished from sight.

> Tear-filled mother,
> rain in your hair, what sorrow
> do you feed your child?

That afternoon, when we arrived in Auckland, Ned invited me to a party at his house. Scruffs, carefully dressed bohemians, heads of every size, shape and description, they all poured in.

But it was all the wrong mood for me that night. So after a while I went for a walk through the suburban streets. The fragrances of night flowers mixed with the wet dank of winter asphalt. Presently I came across a small park. Seated on a bench, I tried to remember the faces of all the people I had ever met.

Most were now no more than dreams, dreams that had touched me powerfully or weakly, sweetly or distastefully, but all had faded. The only reality was the one which confronted me at this very moment: the wind in the night, the groaning of the trees' branches.

> The sound of a step
> among the wet withered leaves.
> Something? Or nothing?

> The dark trees are large,
> the distant sky is larger,
> yet largest still the – ?

Next morning no one was awake as I stepped over sprawled bodies and made my exit. After buying fruit for breakfast, I began hitching north. But there were few rides. After three hours I found myself in a bus-stop, watching joggers and walkers with their dogs, trying to figure out my next move.

> Past this bus shelter
> there walk so many people,
> never two the same.

But these words didn't capture the full reality. Thinking again, I wrote:

> Past this bus shelter
> there walk so many people,
> never two not the same.

Soon after I caught a ride, and within half an hour was crossing the harbour bridge, headed north. Because it was

Sunday many of the cars were packed with families out for a day trip. By dusk I had reached Whangarei, which offered up a glorious sunset.

> Stood between yesterday
> and tomorrow, who casts this
> shadow on the ground?

The next morning I was lucky enough to be given a ride by a German-born potter named Walter who was travelling all the way to his home in Russell. He had emigrated to New Zealand several years previously after having married Julienne, a New Zealander. With a meal inside me, and the warm family chatter around me, I almost felt like I was home.

> On some magic days
> a quiet self-contained smile
> is a shout to me.

After dinner Walter, his wife Julienne, and I sat together talking and drinking their homemade feijoa wine. They told me about their experiences in Europe, while I in turn described my journey. In response to their request I read some of my poems. Walter then offered to take me the rest of the way in his car the following day. He wouldn't listen to any response other than a thank you.

That night, as I lay in bed, I considered how our life is a journey we each must travel separately, locked as we are in our own individual consciousness, governed by our personal patterns of activity, emotion and thought. So what is it that enables us to feel that we are sharing our existence and that we are all living in the same world?

Above, quiet stars,
the whole world holding its breath.
I lie quiet ... I?

Early the next morning Walter and I hit the road. There was little activity: a farmer herding stock, dogs with hanging tongues, fields where cows grazed. We had decided not to halt until arrival and, after all the days of travelling, suddenly we were there.

Cape Reinga, Aotearoa New Zealand's northernmost point of land. A sea mist clung to the landscape, obscuring our view, although we could hear the crying of seagulls as they swooped in the air currents above.

We stood at a fence, very still, looking into the mist. I thought I could just make out something hovering above the sucking waters. Māori say that when a person dies their spirit leaves their body, travels north to this point, and leaps off to ... wherever spirits go when their time in this world is done.

I tried to capture the feelings of those spirits as they were about to fly off into the unknown. Naturally, I failed. Yet standing there, hearing the cries of the gulls, feeling the mist fingering its way into my heart's soft pulse, I wondered at how strange it is that we are alive and human.

Epilogue

Death is an eventuality which comes to us all. Some say that at its occurrence the true nature of existence will be revealed. Others claim it is possible to discover this reality before we die. If such is the case, then surely that must be the greatest of all journeys.

Thus, far from ending his travels here, this traveller is only just beginning. Yet in this most difficult of undertakings, human hearts are like pebbles in a mountain stream. Sometimes they're frothed by joy and delight; other times they suffer the ice-cold weight of despair. There are moments when we wish to rush ahead, impatiently throwing off everything to lighten our load; at others we feel like the night is so intense that we shall never see dawn. Yet always we wonder if perhaps, around the very next bend ...

Accordingly, this traveller hoists his bag onto his back and lifts his gaze towards whatever waits. In his hands are these pages. He tosses them above his head. From across the seas a wind arrives, picking them up and scattering them high into the air.

With an almost inaudible whisper the sea mist parts and a slight figure slips through to join those already making their way across the water. A ghostly warrior blows a wooden trumpet three times. After the sound dies away, the world surges softly back and the figure disappears into the mist. Leaving the sea to take up again the incessant butt and break of its wash on the coast's rocky shore.

Mira's Tied Bells to Her Ankles —— [1979]

I cannot live without you

Beloved, I cannot live without you.
I long for us to meet, yet what am I to do?

Bloomed lotus without water, night sky with no moon,
I'm a sad woman; lover, when will you return?

Anxious, anguished, I roam lost night and day,
Separation eats my heart, I cry out like one flayed.

Days I feel no hunger, nights I cannot sleep;
When I try to explain I find my tongue won't speak.

Yet what am I to say? Talking's what strangers do.
Lover, come now and fill my being with you!

You own my soul, so why this tortuous absence?
Come to your captive and end this tearful sentence.

Mira has dedicated many lives to you.
She longs to kiss your feet – and prays you want that too!

How is it you're still alive?

Old weeping woman, how is it you're still alive?
Without your beloved Hari, how do you survive?

Because my husband's absent, I've become insane;
Like wood attacked by worms my body has decayed.

There's no medicine which spread will cure these sores;
Nothing has effect when insanity's the cause.

The tortoise lives in the ocean, frogs in ponds and creeks,
Water's their home, in water they grow and beget.

Yet take the fish out of the water and watch with your eyes:
Its body flaps and flops, in a short while it dies.

I roam forest and field to hear the voice of the flute;
My husband is its source, there waits my passion's fruit.

Beloved, Mira holds herself and moans.
This separation hurts – pleasure's in your arms alone!

A bowed head I bring

Krishna! Salutations and a bowed head I bring.

I see you crowned with peacock feathers, forehead marked.
Hair dangles over your ears, on those ears hang rings.

Yes, and you play your flute, it's there on your lower lip.
Just to please Radha, you play melodies with silver wings.

O happy, happy Mira, that she can witness this sight.
Her brimming heart smiles. She claps her hands and sings!

Mira's tied bells to her ankles

Mira's tied bells to her ankles, see how she dances!
There's magic in her feet, and fire in her glances!

Why has such ecstasy into her been poured?
Because she declared herself the servant of the lord!

People stared and shouted she's become insane.
Those of high caste said she brought her house shame.

Ranaji has sent a cup of poison for her to drink.
She drained it with a laugh and didn't even feel sick!

Know Mira's beloved will never not be.
He's eternal delight, and she found him so easily!

Do not leave this love

Friends! Do not go, do not leave this love!

Come together, join me, embracing him with your eyes,
Come and discover what great joy in that vision resides!

See the beauty of Krishna, the ecstasy he gives,
Come see his face, for only then can you say you've lived!

Who cares what shape or name to him you ascribe?
If one path unveils, walk it; whatever works, that try!

Says Mira, not all seekers find what they are looking for.
Only the lucky know the joy of embracing their lord!

Remain before my eyes

Beloved! Please always remain before my eyes.

Enter my vision and there permanently reside.
No, never leave; no forgetting nor chilling goodbyes.

I float on this world's cares without attachments or ties.
Take care of your lover so she never has cause to cry.

Ranaji has sent poison, he wants me to die.
I pray, turn this to a cup of nectar; show I don't lie.

May Mira at last meet the one she most admires.
And may there be no parting after, just love's eternal fire!

I shall dance

I shall dance in the presence of Krishna, my lord.
Purely to please, my bare feet will caress the floor.

So solemn and enticing, I shan't be ignored,
And as I turn, closer – to examine him – will I draw.

Yes, love's tied bells to my ankles, tinkling, so small.
And who knows? Perhaps, as I dance, all my veils will fall.

What do I care for customs and the world's joyless laws?
When he arrives, I shall silently close the door.

Yes, Mira will share her lover's bed, embraced and warm.
They'll laugh and sip love's wine – she knows she won't
      be bored!

Six Portraits ———— [1979–1981]

Travellers

Twelve thirty. An all-night cafe. Smells of coffee and fried food.

The waitress sits behind the counter, her hair tinted purple by the light of the electric fly-exterminator hanging overhead. She is staring into the quiet street outside. The only movement is provided by the cafe's red neon blinking ... -OFFEE ... -OFFEE ... -OFFEE ... She looks back inside, across the room, at the faded travel poster that pictures Bali. Beneath it sit a man and woman, the only customers. They have been there for some time, alternatively talking and lapsing into silence. They are silent now.

The waitress picks up a cigarette from the ashtray under the counter, draws on it, and puts it back. Exhaling smoke, she begins filing her nails. But from the corners of her eyes she watches the couple. They are hunched over the table, eyes meeting then parting, meeting, parting. She shifts her attention to the window. It is dirty, smeared with fingerprints and the dust and fumes of passing cars. She takes a last pull on the cigarette, extinguishes it in the ashtray, stands, and walks out into the back of the cafe.

Closing the toilet door behind her, she pulls down her pants and sits. Paint is peeling from the back of the door. She picks at it idly with a finger-nail, then puts her elbows on her knees and rubs her eyes with the heels of her hands. Looking down tiredly at the chipped black and white floor tiles, she lets out a long sigh. A car revs throatily in the street behind the cafe, followed by the sound of a woman's laugh. The car drives off in a squeal of tires.

It takes two pulls on the chain to make the toilet flush. The mirror above the hand basin reflects her face as she dries her hands. There are dark rings under her eyes. She leans forwards and touches a small pimple forming on her chin, then glances into the cafe. The couple have started talking again, but the sound of the refilling toilet cistern drowns their words.

Letting the hand-towel fall on its string, she walks across the back room to the telephone balanced on top of an open packet of serviettes, picks up the receiver, and dials a number. The phone rings. Time passes. The phone keeps ringing. More time passes.

She gently puts down the telephone receiver and stands staring at it. Gradually, she becomes aware of the sound of gushing water. The toilet is still flushing. Going in, she lifts the cistern lid and pulls the jammed float free. Immediately the flushing stops and the cistern begins to fill. She dries her hand on the hand towel, takes an unopened packet of cigarettes out of the shoulder bag hanging on a hook beside the basin, and walks back out into the cafe.

The couple fall silent as the waitress's stool scrapes on the floor. The man glances up at her as she sits. She unwraps the cellophane from the cigarette packet, sees him watching her, and stares back. He looks away. She picks a match from the ashtray and probes her ear with the unused end. After examining the wax, she puts the matchstick back in the ashtray and stares out the window again. But she's not looking outside. She's observing the couple's reflection in the glass.

They sit, silent. The man toys with his empty coffee cup. The woman stares at him. His eyes meet hers briefly. He looks away.

The waitress picks up the nail-file and starts filing the nails on her other hand.

Bang!

The waitress' eyes flick across to the man as he stands abruptly, the chair bouncing on the floor behind him. He stares down at the woman. She glares back.

'Fine.' He bends down to pick up the chair. His hands are shaking as he puts it back under the table. 'Fine,' he repeats. 'Fine.'

He turns and walks towards the door. However, when he reaches it he hesitates, turns to look back. The woman is staring at the wall in front of her. He stares at her briefly. She doesn't move. He sighs, turns into the darkness, and walks off down the street. Still the woman doesn't move.

The waitress puts down the file and takes out a bottle of nail polish from under the counter. As she shakes it the woman stands, picks her bag off the table, and walks to the door. She walks in the direction opposite to that taken by the man. Her footsteps fade into the night.

Unhurriedly, the waitress unscrews the polish container's lid, puts colour on the brush, and paints a single stroke on her thumb-nail. She holds it out at arm's length, examining the effect.

Bzzzz! A fly strikes the grill of the electric fly-exterminator and bursts into flame.

She glances up, watches until the flame burns out. Then she takes a piece of gum out of her pocket, puts it into her mouth and, chewing slowly, begins to paint her nails.

A Song for Sandra

It was a night in June.
We felt the frost and the moon
fell across our bed,
casting shadows on all we said,
on the false promises we made
so one night longer pain was delayed.

And Sandra missed the train.
She stood in the dark and the rain
beat upon her face.
She disappeared without a trace
that day after she rang on the phone.
Who knew she felt so alone?

Bill was more than he seemed.
We felt his force and his dreams
haunted our brief words.
He was the only one who heard
that time Sandra said she was damned.
Perhaps that was what she planned.

But it was you she choose
to hide behind, and the pose
of one who knew what she wanted,
of one who was undaunted,
she made us think was what she was:
everything she gained she lost.

I saw you yesterday.
I wish I had the words
to say you acted well.

But Sandra that cold night
heard the wind and fell
in solitude, in fright.
Yes, and I was full of hell
for that poor wounded girl
you took into your bed,
and kissed by candlelight.

You and I, we have our shame.
Our tears are dry and the stain
bleaches our bleak hearts.
When we are near we are apart.
Love's a bargain we shouldn't waive,
but we're not among the brave.

So here we are again,
deep in the dark and the rain
will not stop tonight.
The weak do not know how to fight.
I wish I could learn to be free,
like the wind that wraps around the trees.

The Soldier

The orders came late summer,
the sun burnt through the sky;
my brothers opened the orders
and wiped the sweat from their eyes.
They left us the next morning
after mumbling short goodbyes.
I waved to them my kisses
as the dark clouds sailed on by.

    And that night I dreamed I saw him,
    the soldier dressed in brown.
    In the moonlight he looked handsome:
    I didn't make a sound.

We listened to the radio
as we waited for the dawn.
The dark was close around us,
the curtains were not drawn.
Mother cried for father
who died when I was born.
The news detailed our retreat,
while the distant bombs fell down.

    And the soldier strode the hilltop,
    where all the shadows run.
    He slowly turned and saw me.
    I wanted him to come.

The troops arrived next morning.
They set the farm on fire.
They asked where were the others,
then said I was a liar.

Mother was shot later,
I was tied with wire.
When I woke I was bleeding;
I washed my body and cried.

    And the soldier stood near to me.
    His face was slightly frowned.
    The twilight fell across us.
    I put on my wedding gown.

In the distance guns were shooting,
I heard footsteps in the hay.
The darkness flashed and thundered,
then they slowly went away.
I shivered in the shadows
until the moonlight came.
My soldier stood in the ruins:
their smoke was cold and grey.

    And his hands were kind and gentle.
    His eyes were warm and brown.
    In the solitude he kissed me.
    I didn't make a sound.

Peter's Story

When the door behind me closed
the wind pulled at my ruffled clothes.
I shivered once and moved my feet,
their footsteps loud through empty streets.
From the doorways shadows ran
across my heart like clutching hands.
I vowed I wouldn't shed a tear,
not now that love had disappeared.
How come we dream our love won't die?
How come we shrug and clutch our lies?
Claim the gaze which peers round bends
doesn't herald the coming end?
When first we met he squeezed my hand;
I blushed and returned his stare.
That night we whispered long in bed.
But this will be the last affair.

Out of the night sirens burned
distant warnings where neons turn.
I frowned and quickly turned away,
into a dim but warm cafe.
The bitter coffee bit my tongue,
the other tables sat but one:
a drunk lost in his sodden stare,
mouthing yarns to what was not there.
Once I was drunk, just like him,
mistaking soul for what was skin.
I won't make that mistake again:
life from now won't be the same.
Tonight he couldn't find a start.
I smiled to cover up my fear.
I know we always vow the worst,
but this will be the last affair.

Sal's Tattoo

No-one walks around here now,
the bums have all gone away.
No cigarettes are burning now
among the glasses and ashtrays.
That's the piano in the corner,
it came from the old Savoy.
I've played a few sweet songs on her,
tickled a tune for the boys.
And there's where Charlie laid his head,
the night his missus locked him out.
She never let him in again:
Charlie said that was worth a shout.
Funny how the times roll past,
they're gone before you know.
Now I've got the floor for a bed,
burnt-out butts for a pillow.
And all those voices, faces and yarns,
all those songs we used to sing,
they kind of fade away right now,
like the taste of discount gin.

Yeah, this bar had something special,
something that made it right.
Sure we had our moments,
but we outdrank a fair few nights.
That corner's where bald Max sat,
he was always good for a laugh.
And that's whining Tommy's spot;
his wife drowned in the bath.
Where have the boys all got to now?
Where's Copper and Whiskey and Stud?
Seems it was only yesterday
we were passing round the jug.

Maybe I will have that bottle, buddy,
just one more for old times.
The way this overcoat's thinning out
I need something to warm my insides.
Cause all those voices, faces and yarns,
all those lies we used to tell,
they kind of fade away right now,
like some tolling church-house bell.

Hey, that's the old brass hat-stand,
there below the broken neon lights.
Cobwebs hang on all those tubes now,
they were such a pretty sight.
Remember that day in 'sixty-nine
when Bill got his new false teeth?
The way they looked on top of the bar:
yeah, those times were so complete.
And that's where Joe and Frankie tussled.
Strange, I can't think what they broke.
I sure am feeling cold,
and that ceiling's come mighty close.
No, don't you worry none for me,
just put your mouth to my ear,
cause though I see your lips moving,
your voice is too soft to hear.
And all those voices, faces and yarns,
all those tales we used to spin,
they kind of fade away right now,
like the taste of discount gin.
Yeah, all those voices, faces and yarns,
all those songs we used to sing,
they kind of fade away right now,
fade away into the wind.

Islands

Walking. Past pieces of driftwood. Past dunes and a withered pine trunk. As the sun sinks between two distant islands and a lone gull flies crying back and forth across the bay.

They stop. Foam sucks at their feet. Orange light falls from the sky. And they hug each other as they watch. They are in love. They are together. They are alone.

From the land behind a faint breeze stirs, gentle at first, but soon pushing, urging them out to the islands, now black bulks against the darkening sky.

The woman shivers. 'Let's go in now.'

Their discarded clothes fall in a heap. Hand in hand they plunge into the water. Skin bristles where foam splashes and cool air bites. A wait until the next wave breaks. Then both are under, thrown and sundered, rolled by turbulence, in darkness and helplessness, wetness and a shortage of air.

Coughing and spluttering, heads above water and laughing, they rejoin in the calm beyond the breaking waves' line. Fingers link eagerly. Bodies rub electrically. And the warm sea caresses their skins, licking the long line from throat to toe. They feel free.

The two islands rise from the ocean. Clouds form a thin line between them, to either side of them. Their presence is a calling. He feels the urge.

'Race you,' he whispers.

And pulling himself free strikes out.

'No!'

He makes a few more strokes, halts, treads water.

'It's not far,' he says.

'Liar.'

He eyes the islands, shrugs, slowly starts back.

'Race you!' she shouts.

And her panting is drowned in the thrill of their splashing.

He catches her in the foam, locks his arms around her, tumbling and shrieking, panting and choking. Water surges around them. They wrestle into stillness. Her body moulds to his as he kisses her lips.

They lie in the shallows, washed by waves, catching their breaths. Day is a pleasure, but night is their joy time. The air tingles with the memory of what lies ahead.

As one they rinse the sand from their hair and run up the beach to their clothes. Wrapped in a towel they stand among the dunes, faces buried in each other's shoulder.

From behind the clouds a crescent moon emerges, illuminating with icy light the islands and the pair who embrace so fervently on the strip of sand which separates ocean from land.

Gently, they lie down. Softly, they kiss. Quietly, they sigh. And their motion merges with the rolling waves' hiss. While high above the moon rises free of the clouds and serenely sails through the black sky.

By degrees the pair still themselves. Turned on their backs, they watch the moon. Listen to the waves. Feel the dark press around them. She runs her fingers through his wet hair. He caresses the salt from her breasts. Their warm breaths mingle. They are content.

Beyond the beach, beyond the breaking waves, the two islands stand as they have for thousands of years. Somewhere around their cliffs a seagull lets out a single shriek. Nothing moves. For just this moment nothing answers.

But soon two figures will be walking.

Exile and Return _____ [1981]

The slave reviews his situation

Here, in this foreign land, soulless and enslaved, I toil;
in the temple of Baal, I serve those called royal.

What holiness: the temple walls are smeared with blood!
And purity: they kill virgins and swear unending love!

Yahweh, Nebuchadnezzar and his priests are a blight.
How much longer must I be slave to their cruel spite?

I know your prophets proclaim him your servant too,
but he vilifies your name, inverting the truth.

'Submit to Baal,' he said, daring we deny our Lord.
Jerusalem denied him – and suffered his sword.

Our people gathered in the temple; they came at dawn;
by evening the survivors were too shocked to mourn.

Jerusalem, when night fell you were cast in shade;
your people were bound and marched to Babylon, enslaved.

Yahweh, your slaves weep, having suffered a great fall.
With them I wait, sorrowful, for your releasing call.

The slave's lament

Yahweh, could you possibly have forgotten me?
Then why I am Babylon's slave, still locked in her see?

How long is it now? My feet say too great a time:
I trudge these dusty streets, but my heart longs for the sky.

I hate Babylon: each day I pray for escape.
My lips crack, my throat rasps, but still you hide your face.

My Lord, how much longer must I look and not see?
The sheep have pasture, the swallows nests – yet observe me!

My home's Jerusalem, but you have trapped me here.
All day, like jackals, our captors bite our heels and jeer.

Yahweh, where now is your merciful power to save?
You brought us from Egypt, gave us manna: we obeyed.

How you inspired Moses! Opened up the Red Sea!
Dealt death to those who were Zion's enemy!

We listened when you said, 'Worship no foreign gods.'
I have no other, yet I'm treated worse than their dogs!

At least a dog's warmed by the fire, given a bone;
But I am whipped and abused, I fear I'm alone.

Yahweh, I've forgotten what it is to be free.
All I feel is the vile curse of the enemy.

The slave remembers

And there I sat, by the waters of Babylon.
I sat and I wept, as I remembered Zion.

Disconsolate, alone, my heart reached out for death.
I hung my harp on a willow, and I bent my head.

Drunk, they cried, 'Sing us a song of your homeland,
sing of how your Lord's strength helps you command.'

And I put my head in my hands, I made no reply.
I hid my face from them so none could hear me cry.

Yahweh, I don't heed them, my heart is pledged to you;
they're vultures and carrion, but you will lift me through.

What do they know? Their breath stinks of their drunkeness.
I could never sing to you in their vile presence.

My Jerusalem! When I think of her I shiver.
If ever I forget her, may my right hand wither.

Yahweh, you remember how they laughed at your laws;
yes, and how they spat on Jerusalem's pure walls.

This daughter of Babel's a whore, return her mock.
Take her! Crush her! Throw her children screaming on the rock!

Yahweh you are my Lord, my song is for you alone.
They will never hear me sing, never of Zion, my home.

The slave longs for his lover

Last night, on my bed, I sought you whom my heart loves.
In the moonlight, insensible, my heart gushed with blood.

When I lost you in the desert march, yes, I wept.
My eyes blurred and I stumbled, my fractured feet bled.

So it was, last night, that desolation swept my heart.
Once again I felt the anguish of our being far apart.

I rose and walked, I sang to the moon in the sky.
The night watchmen started: I soothed them with a sigh.

Longing, inspired, I flew high above Babylon's streets;
I glimpsed a wadi where sky and horizon meet.

And I thought: There! That is where my beloved waits!
That is the destination to which I must escape!

Then I sank down onto my bed, overcome with bliss.
And I dreamed – wonderful! – I dreamed I felt your kiss.

Daniel instructs the slave

He entered the temple at noon: his eyes flashed in the sun.
I was praying and sweeping; my shirt was all undone.

He said, 'Follow me,' and led me into the streets.
We walked from the market, sat down, and washed our feet.

There he showed me the secret teaching of the heart,
the teaching whereby the seeker soars far apart.

I said, 'I praise and thank you for what you have taught.
Yet still I'm Babylon's slave, still I'm chained and caught.'

He said, 'The Beast will one day receive what is just.
He will die, and our enemies will kiss the dust.

'But until then you must be upright in all you do.
Be a lamp: let peace and light in your heart accrue.

'Remember Yahweh and nothing can harm your peace.
That is the only way for you to find release.'

And he left me then to struggle and to grow strong:
I understood my faith was neither misplaced nor wrong.

Yahweh, you're the merciful conveyor of my fate.
Thank you for Daniel's words: soon I shall escape!

The slave addresses his lover

Don't imagine I have forgotten you, my love:
my heart, remembering you, always pounds with blood.

When dawn lights my bed, I see too well what I'm without;
come dusk, I miss the feel of your kisses on my mouth.

I desire you, not Babylon's passions or wealth,
for without your presence I know I am not myself.

When street women approach me, I just turn away.
You are my heart's whole meaning: what more can I say?

Babylon is brackish water, your lips pure wine;
each evening I pray that you will again be mine.

Each dawn I hold your image in my despairing breast,
longing for your warmth, your perfume, your breath.

Puck of the Starways  [1981]

Preface

The sons and daughters of the Earth live in a wild and frightful world. It is a world of cataclysm and violence, of mystery and seeming unfathomableness, in which life is born painfully and all too suddenly curtailed. So it is now, and so it has been for ages since.

Yet life was not always so.

There once was a time when contentment and bliss animated all, when no shadows fell across any pleasures, and when all were satisfied and content. So far was this era from the world humanity at present occupies that it was called the Land of the Happy. And a wonderful and extraordinary time it was, too.

Then magic wafted on the sunbeams. Then fairies played in the fields, and giants walked the Earth. In that time, humankind lived lives as frivolous and light as the breeze which skips over the flowers and sends their heads nodding gently from side to side. They ate and drank with little thought of what they were or how they came to be. They were as ripples on the surface of the pond. And they sought no more.

But there was more. Much more.

For any world has within it another world, and is itself part of a larger world which embraces it from without. Just so, those living in the Land of the Happy had no conception of the world which resided in their own breasts. And, similarly, they did not know the greater world which encompassed them, of which they and their land formed an infinitesimal part.

Those in the Land of the Happy saw only the shimmering of the fields, and the towering of the mountains. Heard only the sighing of the wind, and the calling of the beasts. Felt only the warmth of the days, and the companionship of the night fire. Smelt only the fresh dawn rising out of night mists, and the coolness of the gurgling streams. Tasted only the sweetness of their food, and the joy which coated all they did with honey. What they experienced, they experienced truly. But their experience was limited. For never did they know the Gods who ruled their world. But those Gods knew them.

High above the Gods resided, beyond the tallest peak. To reach their abode a journey of vast distances was required, into the sky, past the Sun, and through a realm of galaxy upon galaxy, star-host upon star-host. This was the world of the Starways, the abode of the Gods.

Before the Earth was created, the Starways were ancient. And long after the Earth has vanished back into the Sun's fire the Starways will continue to administer over their allotted portion of creation. So the Inconceivable who created the All and Everything ordained it. And so it is still.

The Gods who occupied the Starways were intangible Gods. Unencumbered by bodies, they observed what they observed, and they did what they did. Mysterious are the ways of the Gods now, and mysterious were the ways of the Gods then.

Yet other beings inhabited the Starways, beings who were not themselves Gods, yet who lived in harmony with them, and whose presence was imbued with something of their mystery. Such a one of these lesser beings was Puck.

Day in and day out, never resting, Puck played. Having no body, he flitted from star to star, solar system to solar system. Ever at fun, he gambolled through the ten thousand veils of reality. Life to him was a joy, and that joy was his life's whole meaning.

However, when It created the All and the Everything, the Inconceivable also created the law of change. Nothing within creation escapes its consequences.

And so it was for Puck. He whose time-span was measured in units far exceeding an earthly aeon found that, in the end, he also could not escape time. And thus one day a message came to him from the very centre of the Starways. That message was a command.

'Puck, the Gods require you.'

So away flew Puck. Away through the stars, away through clouds of solar systems wherein each system was as a speck of dust, and each speck hid ten million others. Faster than light he flashed through the Starways. And in a moment he was in the presence of the Gods.

The Gods of the Starways were awesome beings, existing far beyond the imagination's power to conceive of them. Their power resided in an intangible potency which, because formless, meant they could fill any part of the All and Everything with their dread presence. Yet they lived in hiddenness, apart.

Puck was a toy compared to their vastness. And a toy Puck felt as he stood in their midst. Sensing their profound power, he could not but tremble. So tremble he did.

And the Gods of the Starways spoke to Puck.

'Puck, your days of play have ended. Now you must enter into the activities of the Gods.'

Puck bowed low and listened.

'Puck,' said the Gods, 'there is another world of which you know nothing. This world exists far from the Starways. It is called the Land of the Happy. By the decree of the Inconceivable, we Gods of the Starways watch over it. For many aeons the Land of the Happy has been true to its name. But everything changes. And now doubt and pain have entered the lives of those who dwell there. Go to the Land of the Happy, Puck. On behalf of the Gods, go and discover why this is so.'

Puck bowed again before the overwhelming Gods.

And when he straightened, he discovered he was plunging away, out of the Starways, down through the ten thousand veils of reality, out of the regions of light, through the realms of time and space, into a different region altogether, of sights, sounds, and colours.

Ever faster he travelled, until a cacophony of impressions flooded him and, for a moment, he lost awareness of who, where or what he was.

The Man Who Would Be Wise

When Puck returned to himself he found he was in a world very different from the Starways. Green fields stretched into the distance. Beyond them forests of enormous and graceful trees rose high into an intense blue sky. And even further away stood the huge masses of mountains, their peaks sprinkled with snow.

Puck stood gazing at them for a long time, marvelling that such a world could exist. And as he did he came to realise that he *was* standing. Curious, he looked down at the body which surrounded him. And he smiled.

For, in sending him into the Land of the Happy, the Gods had given him the body of a youth whose limbs were filled with boundless energy. He stretched. He jumped. He ran.

But for only a short time. Because he was soon drawn to consider his task. Somewhere, somehow, doubt and pain had entered the Land of the Happy. And he was commanded to find it.

So away Puck went. Swift as the wind, as lightly as a leaf, Puck skipped over the grasses and began a reconnaissance. And, as he did, he gained his first view of the beings who lived in the Land of the Happy.

Small villages he passed, housing just a few people, several shouting children, one or two smiling elderly folk, a flock of goats and sheep. Through larger villages he flitted, wherein many families lived and worked contentedly together. By lonely outposts he sped, where only one or two existed in laughter and happiness.

And everywhere Puck went, he saw only satisfaction. Nowhere was there doubt, or despair, or pain. For these were the days before disease or famine, when work was small and not laborious, when the elements created no hardships, and when death came gently, as a wafting breeze in the night. Such was life to these people. They were as a ripple on the surface of a pond. And they sought no more.

As the days passed, then the weeks, Puck grew ever more skillful. Sometimes he took on the body of the beautiful youth he possessed when he first arrived. But at other times he became an elderly man, lame and prophetic, or a farmer who could read the clouds. Sometimes he became a woman, warm and maternal, and sometimes a bent grandmother who spat often and cursed small children for their noises, yet understood the secrets of herbs and plants.

Sometimes he even bypassed the human form altogether and became a crow flying high over humankind's heads. Or he changed into a deer that hovered tremulously at the edge of the forest, and when human beings approached leapt into the undergrowth.

Yet he never forgot the task the Gods had given him. Somewhere, one in the Land of the Happy was sad. And it was Puck's challenge to find who this person was.

And so it was that Puck heard talk of one who was sad and lived by himself on the edge of the ocean. It was a passing wonder among the people. A man who could be sad in the Land of the Happy, they observed. How could that be? Yet this was just another wonder among many.

For there was the wonder of the sun rising each day. And the wonder of the birds which danced and swooped through the air. And the wonder of the world around them which grew so colourful and lovely. And it passed among these other wonders and was lost. But not to Puck.

Swifter than the breeze which runs and tumbles, head over heels, across the tops of the trees, he flashed to the edge of the ocean. And there he found that one in the Land of the Happy who was sad.

The man was seated on a rock on the beach, looking out over the waves, which beat one after the other, endlessly, on the shore. His eyes were the most mournful Puck had yet seen in his adventures in the Land of the Happy.

Puck stepped towards him.

'Hello,' Puck said. 'I've come a very long way to see you.'

The man should have been startled. But he was so numbed that he did not even look up. Instead he shrugged and kept his eyes on the waves.

'You are unique,' Puck said. 'You are sad when everyone else is happy. Why is that?'

Still the man remained silent.

'I will not leave until you answer.'

The waves continued to lap onto the shore. At last, the man opened his mouth and replied.

'I am sad,' he said, 'because I am not wise.'

Puck was astonished. That is, he was as astonished as a being from the Starways could be.

'What do you mean, you are not wise?'

The man picked up a piece of wood and threw it onto the water. Together, they watched it bob on the waves.

'We are like that driftwood. We float on the surface of life, never able to glimpse the depths. But I wish to see those depths. That is what I mean when I say I am not wise. And because I know I shall never see them, I have become sad.'

'How can you say that?' Puck objected. 'Look around you. See what a wonderful world you live in. The breeze is blowing, the waves are lapping, the sea-birds are calling, the sand is warm. You have food and shelter. You have all you need. How can this not be sufficient for you and your kind?'

Finally, the man looked up.

'All that is true,' he said sharply. 'This world is happy. And we are alive. Yet we are ignorant. People say we are ruled by the Gods. Perhaps this is true. But I don't see them. Where are they? Do we live in their light? Or is this land the crumbs they left behind when they departed? It is cruel for the Gods to keep us in ignorance. Either let us be wise as they must be. Or let death stamp on us and end our existence forever. For I cannot endure this situation even one day longer.'

Puck was enjoying this conversation immensely. 'Surely you don't wish to die before your time!'

'If I remain ignorant, it makes no difference whether I die to-day, or tomorrow, or a thousand years hence. In the end it is all the same. Emptiness and nothing.'

And with that the man closed his eyes, lowered his head onto his arms, and would speak no more.

Ten thousand thoughts raced through Puck's mind. Could it be as it appeared? Could this man really crave wisdom? Is wisdom even something human beings might be capable of possessing?

Puck knew what he needed to do. So he called out the secret name of the Gods.

Immediately, he felt himself being lifted out of his body, into the skies, then pulled past the Sun, through the hidden doorway, and back into the world which is the Starways. Once again, great presences surrounded the diminutive Puck. Once again, he bowed low before the Gods.

'Puck,' commanded the Gods, 'report your findings.'

'I went to the Land of the Happy,' he said. 'I found the one there who is sad. And I discovered the reason for his sadness.'

'And what is his reason?' asked the Gods.

'The man is sad,' Puck responded, 'because he is not wise.'

And around him Puck felt the Gods rejoicing. Their titanic laughter shook the Starways. Their satisfaction redounded through the ten thousand veils of reality. Their tears watered a million worlds. And Puck stood in their midst, and wondered.

'Puck,' said the Gods when they had completed their rejoicing, 'we have waited aeon after aeon for one from the Land of the Happy to say what you have just told us. We are elated. For when the Inconceivable created the All and the Everything, It hid wisdom in a special place. It buried that place deep within the ten thousand veils of reality. And It proclaimed that nothing of value should be easily obtained. Accordingly, only those who search and struggle will find wisdom. But there will be frustration, too. And emptiness and pain of lack. And even, at times, suffering. So return to the Land of the Happy, Puck. Return and tell that one who is sad that if he wants wisdom for himself and for his people, the price to be paid is struggle, frustration, emptiness, pain, and suffering.'

Away flashed Puck. And in a trice he found himself back on the shore, standing in front of the man who was sad.

But this time the man was standing too, an astonished expression on his face. For he had seen Puck appear from out of the air. And that meant he was in the company of one who was not of this world. He threw himself on his knees.

'Forgive me! How could I know you were of the Gods.'

Puck smiled.

'I am merely a messenger of the Gods. They have replied to your complaint that you lack wisdom. Know that they are pleased with your sentiment. But there is a price to be paid for the acquisition of wisdom. For only those who struggle can achieve wisdom.'

The man was ecstatic. 'I can see there must be a price. I am more than content with what you say.'

'There is more,' Puck stated. 'The price may be struggle. But struggle does not walk alone. In its shadow slides a feeling of lack. And when lack arrives, so does discontent. Discontent has a cousin, frustration. And where discontent and frustration hold hands, emptiness reigns. Know emptiness carries the knife of suffering. And that knife penetrates the heart. All this means an irreversible change to your existence. Think well on this before you respond.'

But the man could scarcely contain his excitement.

'I understand what you are saying,' he said. 'It is natural that wisdom should have such a price, and that our existence will change irrevocably. But I am content if the Gods have proclaimed that it must be so.'

'The price of wisdom,' Puck continued, 'is that you and all your fellow beings will no longer live in the Land of Happy. Your world will become a land of doubt and heartache and anguish. Unhappiness and pain and misery will stalk you all. And emptiness will fill you. Think it over well. Is this truly what you desire?'

'I don't need to think on that,' the man said. 'Life which is not always happy, which is difficult and hard, yet which contains a purpose, is incomparably better than a life which is easy, yet leads nowhere, and which does not see into the way of things. I accept the will of the Gods. I kneel and assent to their decree.'

And with that the man fell silent. Truly, this was a moment befitting silence. So Puck sat beside him and spoke no more.

But when the sun sank, and the stars came out, and the moon rose, and all in the Land of the Happy soundly slept, Puck called out the secret name of the Gods. And in a moment found himself again in their presence.

'Well, Puck,' demanded the Gods, 'what is your report?'

'I visited the Land of the Happy,' Puck said. 'I spoke to the one there who is sad. And I told him the price of wisdom.'

'That is well done,' said the Gods. 'What is his reply?'

'His reply,' said Puck, 'is that if feelings of dissatisfaction, lack, frustration and suffering are the price of wisdom, he and his kind are satisfied to pay it.'

And again the Gods rejoiced. Again their pleasure echoed through the Starways. Again their tears washed ten million worlds. And the God's made their proclamation.

'We Gods are not spiteful Gods. We carry out only what the Inconceivable has ordained. And It has ordained that the sons and daughters of the Earth must do as they shall do, and be as they shall be, in order to become wise. Yet when they are wise, they will take their places among us. And we will share our duties with them joyfully, for that is what the Inconceivable decreed when It created the All and the Everything. So go now, Puck. Return to the Land of the Happy. Return to the sons and daughters of the Earth and help them as you are able. Surely, they will need your aid and guidance, and all our collective love and compassion. For that is as the Inconceivable has arranged their existence. Now go.'

Puck bowed.

Then down he flew, down to the Land of the Happy. But when he reached there, he saw it was the Land of the Happy no more. For the Gods of the Starways had spoken truly. They had done what the Inconceivable decreed they should do.

They had removed contentment. They had withdrawn happiness. They had ended whatever satisfaction the Earth's sons and daughters had previously felt with what floated on life's surface. And they had replaced it with a longing for something more.

Now shadows strode across the Land of the Happy. Now, all was not peaceful. All was no longer harmonious. Broils broke out. Fights and wars. Diseases ate holes in bodies. And sickness and despair attacked all without distinction.

Now Death stalked in daylight. And he no longer took people gently. Instead, he wielded a scythe. And where he plundered, there was an aftermath of lamentation. Where before people had laughed without thinking, now they tried not to think. And when they did think, they wept.

And the Gods created the villages of Er and Orr. And they filled the Sea of Desolation with the madness of the Moon. And from the Moon's shadow they created the Mountains of What Cannot Be. And on one side of those Mountains they shaped the Valley of the Never Was. While on the far side they laid out the Desert Plain.

And in the middle of the Desert Plain they sat Sorrow, who wept day and night, without cessation. And from Sorrow's tears they formed a river.

And that river they directed to flow through the vales which suckled all those who lived in the Land of the Happy. And whoever drank of that river went mad. And there was none alive who, at some time during their life, did not drink thereof.

Yet the Gods were not malicious in their intent. They wished only the best for all charges. And to show their compassion, they left sparkles of sunlight in that shadowy world, as reminders of what could be experienced when humankind achieved wisdom. So none suffered all the time, but rather experienced flashes of happiness which briefly illuminated their lives. Those flashes may have been infrequent. Yet they were passionately remembered, and were clung to long after they had passed.

Pinched by lack, battered by despair, some viewed those flashes as a divine joke, given by the Gods that the sons and daughters of the Earth might suffer the more. Yet in others, who experienced dissatisfaction, emptiness, discontent, and lack, there gradually developed an understanding that the Gods were kind in doing so. And they took those flashes as they were meant, as gifts to be used for celebration.

And this was how the Land of the Happy was transformed into to the Land of the Sad.

Yet all were not sorrowful in that altered world. For that one who had asked the Gods to act so was far from discontent. In the Land of the Sad, there was now one who was happy. Such irony was not lost on those who observed it.

And such irony has accompanied the sons and daughters of the Earth ever since.

Poems of Light and Love

——— [1981–1983]

That which reason never

That which reason never thought of has captured me;
that which thought is distraught at has enraptured me.

Like a nighthawk love swooped one evening through the dark:
I was knocked over and it made off with my heart.

Who can tell the mystery love's stealing invokes?
I have and I don't have, I'm a wheel without spokes.

Ecstasy and pain mingle madly in my breast:
rushing here, sitting there, I'm in peace while distressed.

The gnostic both loves, and doesn't love, his ecstasy.
Does this sound strange? Yet that's his ambiguity.

This knowing, this unknowing, it's the language of the soul;
the lover seeks it, but it's beyond their control.

The world is not alive until love fills your heart.
Silence! Words are chains, and love calls us to depart!

From the unseen

(After Rumi)

From the unseen, the secret of love is coming;
from the gracious depths, the beloved's scent is coming.

Everywhere hearts reject what is unbecoming;
to the hungry the father's call is coming.

Heaven's manna has always been forthcoming,
reality's vault has never seen more running.

On love's path the seekers have set their feet drumming:
from non-being to being the lovers are coming.

Every one is silent, for the call is not loud;
every one listens, for it is easily drowned.

Clean out your ear if you are unable to hear,
for though you are deaf, yet that voice is so near.

Human voices are sweet, yet their fruit is numbing,
but now the master of eternal bliss is coming.

Silence! The sound of your voice is tuneless strumming:
the maker of the lover's tongue is coming.

The world is laughing

The world is laughing, dawn dances through the trees,
birds chatter morning madness, joy pulls on the leaves.

The grass is singing, meadows moan an ancient song,
the dancing flowers bow, on breezes sweet scents throng.

The whole wide world is trembling, filled with flitting wings,
the sky echoes their beating, all wonder what they bring.

Sorrow exits with shadows, peace spreads across the world,
hearts open like shells, love intoxicates her pearls.

The call to leave resounds, wings hammer in the ear,
creatures tremble with bliss, something other is near.

Ecstasy's arrived, it heralds profound release;
all quiver with inward joy, feeling love's sweet peace.

Put an end to speaking, let no coarse sounds remain;
whatever is left unsaid, love itself will explain.

That mad milkman

That mad milkman has come smashing bottles again!
That milk-shedding lip is dispersing joyousness again!

Open your mouth, drink deep of soulfulness, my friend;
reason has fallen, we ride the flood to the end.

The sky has broken and love immerses us again;
intoxication takes us out of ourselves, my friend.

Do not turn away, for that would surely offend;
the unquenched heart weeps for what it can't comprehend.

Hold back your tongue, words must not confuse, my friend;
on a silent wave mysteries embrace us again.

Do not cry, "Enough!", for that pouring has no end;
better to drown than allow our longing to bend.

Silence! Words are but metaphors our experiences transcend,
for that one has merged his heart with our heart once again.

Don't let religion

My friends, don't let religion persuade you to be sad.
You seek the joyful, so why make yourself feel bad?

The religion of sin makes the heart sick and unwell;
its poor converts tremble between heaven and hell.

But what is our purpose? For what task were we born?
Do we seek the rose? Then why embrace the thorn?

When ecstasy enters there's no room left for sin;
it empties out the house, then lights it from within.

Its embrace is a fire that burns all else away;
forget tomorrow's hopes and fears – it's here today!

The religion of love is beyond evil and good:
lovers live what they know, not as books say they should.

But words are insufficient, look into your heart;
love's subtle secret only it, there, can impart.

There is a tremor

There is a tremor in the night, a warmth in the air,
a gentleness in the heart, and a whisper in the ear.

There are secrets arrived, there are silence and love,
there are calm passions present, and tidings from above.

Peace has entered, departed the proddings of pain,
contentment has entered, and the heart no longer craves.

All is at rest, great blessings pillow the soul,
the beloved's hand descends and comforts as it holds.

The lover is embraced, surrounded by the all,
the all echoes within and the heart is enthralled.

Everything is quiet, the body makes no sound,
love walks in silence and presents what is profound.

Lovers want for nothing, they're neither happy nor sad;
something else has arrived, and in that are they clad.

This crazed parrot

(After Rumi)

This crazed parrot is intoxicated again;
this ecstatic bird is flapping its cage again.

A secret sugar was brought by love's emissary;
now, by that sweetness, its heart is enamoured again.

Amazing! How light focuses the eye that was so bleary.
Amazing! That accident gives way to the necessary.

Radiance explodes, causing the hard bars to bend;
because of that cause, tears start from the heart again.

In the chest's well ecstatic blood is bubbling again,
in this river happiness is raging again.

This fever's neither yellow nor small, like the canary;
this passion's an eagle flying the unseen again.

Love called and it straight returned to being's aerie,
to reality it flew, far from non-being's prairie.

Amazing! Love has begun to frolic, my friends:
from the unseen to the seen she leaps, then back again.

This is a tale whose reciting knows no end,
for, on my ear, love herself is pulling once again!

Compassion falls

The sky is crying, compassion falls like soft rain;
one single drop and we each join love's splintered train.

Who has seen the tree explode? The eye is much too pale:
open up the heart and the 'I' becomes a sail.

On the seas of sorrow the body's far too slow;
the 'I' wants only storms, for fierce winds to blow.

The hurricane rages, nothing stands in its path,
yet when all forms are shattered something stands at last.

That something is singing, you can hear it here and now;
don't listen with the ear, make your 'I' into a bow.

Slicing through the sensual, the heart rises above:
the unseen is singing, its only message is love.

Scuttle the ship, stand the frothing world on its head,
the true sailor is the one at the wheel who's dead.

Something has touched me

Something has touched me, something difficult to name;
it caught me suddenly and made my heart feel strange.

I was laughing with friends, abruptly those laughs slowed,
detachment entered, but tinged with gentle sorrow.

A feeling both heavy and light now fills my heart:
slowly it wells, silently, drawing me apart.

It is something I feel, but no 'I' is the subject,
a calm passion, yet without particular object.

It is a flowing from above to the heart below;
once enhoused, it laterally spreads its subtle glow.

All are both subject and object of its embrace,
for while bodies swing, the spirit has another estate.

There are many troubles, many trials and pains:
we choose our own path each moment of night and day.

What is your face?

What is your face? For what reason do you change?
You own ten thousand voices, and every one is strange.

Laughter tugs at the mirror, clear eyes cloud in pain;
two eyes, one image: in the puddle oceans rage.

The world's a round-a-bout which circles in a daze;
upside-down it smiles, not knowing that it's crazed.

Love, what are you? Drunken innocent or sly chain?
I have found you in myself, yet you are not contained.

I would abandon my face, my heart's become estranged:
who has both my outside and my inside rearranged?

There is no answer, words leak from the tongue in vain;
as often love appears, so often love's forms change.

In love, truly, many foaming voices are raised:
let this single voice, in silence, slip beneath your waves.

Confessions of an Antipodean Mudlark ——— [1984]

Preface

> 'I, D.L.T Fizzburg, possessing a questionable state of mind, do bequeath this manuscript, *Confessions of an Antipodean Mudlark*, to future generations that they may understand the peculiar existence of their blessed and blighted forebears .... '

So begins the last literary testament of the late Professor D.L.T. Fizzburg, known to his friends as Fizz. For many years Fizz was my learned colleague and valued friend, a circumstance which led to me being asked by the Professor's literary executors to introduce these few pages, the last of his work to be published since his premature, and much grieved, death.

Fizz's career did not reach the heights his brilliance warranted. The peculiarities of his outlook being central to both his lack of career success and the work that follows, I will begin by proceeding directly to the Professor's philosophy. This may be summed up in one word: matterphysics. Fizz's invention, matterphysics is a philosophy that only ever asks one question, whatever the issue or circumstance: Does it matter? Such a question may seem innocuous, but Fizz was not averse to asking it in the most testing circumstances, during meetings with the Dean, graduation ceremonies, weddings, marriage break-ups and funerals.

After years of repeating what (very soon) became a one-line joke, Fizz started giving business cards to visiting academics introducing The Antipodean Institute of Matterphysics. Intrigued, they would ask if they could visit the Institute. Fizz explained that they could not because there was no physical academy. Rather, he preferred to run all courses by correspondence. Of course, this did not mean professors and students communicated by post or e-mail. For the Institute had no students either. How then, his surprised interlocutors would ask, did his Institute function? Fizz's response was always, 'Very smoothly.'

When pressed further, Fizz would explain that the correspondence at the heart of matterphysics involved neither postage, nor the Cambridge School's position that truth should be sought in the correspondence of definite statement to verifiable fact. Rather, matterphysics sought truth in the correspondence between the unlikely and the improbable. This provided the reason the Institute had neither professors nor students: because it was unlikely potential students will have heard of the Institute of Matterphysics, and it was improbable that those who had not heard of it would seek to enrol in its (non-existent) halls.

This anecdote leads us back to the following text, for the inverted reasoning which underpins matterphysics is equally present in these pag

[*This was as far as Professor Antony Engle progressed in writing his gracious and admiring foreword. He was found by university cleaners, slumped over his typewriter, victim of a heart attack, a half-smoked cigar and a bottle of brandy beside him. He will be sadly missed. Unfortunately, he had with him the only copy of Professor's Fizzburg's manuscript, and when his lighted cigar and the pages made contact, the ensuing flames reduced most of the manuscript to ash. Regretfully, we present here the remaining text. – The Editors.*]

An Analysis of Antipodean Spirituality

[The foregoing pages were burnt]

... hence that Antipodeans are heathens will not come as a surprise, particularly not to those who have investigated palaeontology. It is a fact long verified (recorded in print by someone who presumably was present), that man was formed by God out of clay, that woman came from man's rib, that both were filled with God's breath, and that Christ is God's son sent down to save us all. Every civilised country recognises these facts and accordingly has a set of morals governing their lands which are based on the implications of this metaphysic.

But that is only one argument relative to our theme here. For recent centuries have discovered bones of various apelike creatures resembling modern man and woman. The view has consolidated that, in fact, human beings weren't created in the manner described by the Authorised Version at all, that in reality they e-v-o-l-v-e-d. The enlightened are even now engaged in the battle to eradicate such a heretical concept. Just as tenaciously the scientific community throws Darwinian evolution – the new Authorised Version – back at them. Tooth and claw they fight, the one expecting the fittest argument to survive, the other each moment anticipating resolution by divine decree.

This is a truly distressing situation for us ignorant Antipodeans who look to those superior civilised beings for the truth. Yet we have found a way out of this controversy, a way which will prove both sides correct and extend our thesis regarding the spiritual activity of Antipodeans. What is this theory? We will explain.

First, there can be no doubt directed at the Christian version of creation – too many people have believed it for too long for it not to be absolutely and completely true. For, of course, God cannot have allowed His chosen to believe a fairy tale for any length of time at all. Therefore we must accept that the concept of creation is both valid and here to stay.

Yet, in view of the evidence compiled by scientists regarding fossils, the movement of fish from the sea to land, and the development of the Neanderthal, Cro-magnon and Homo sapiens species, the objective observer is forced to admit that the theory of evolution must also be true.

Yet if we accept both arguments, an interesting question arises. What has happened to these two lines? If both survived, who and where are their descendants? Which is actually a simple question to answer. Both lines mingled over the few thousand years they had time to do so. But when the Antipodes was discovered, the created stayed in Europe while those who had evolved from apes immediately boarded ships and set sail for the Antipodes, where they established new homes. For if the colonialists weren't evolved from apes why should they so eagerly wish to live in a rough-hewn land whose only virtue was the great number of trees it possessed? The answer speaks for itself.

Having disposed of that conundrum, we can now see why the Antipodean is a heathen. Being descended from the evolved line, and therefore lacking that God-given spark in his breast, he sees nothing in religion beyond a repetition of social formulae. Thus we return to the argument which opened this essay. Antipodean spirituality is unrefined. Lacking feeling for the depths of religious fervour, Antipodeans don't respect God. While He has been administering corrective retribution on Europe, Asia and the Americas in the form of wars, plagues, disputes, fears, and internal haemorrhaging of the social and economic systems, life in the Antipodes has had to pass on without such blessed concern. The peaceful life which resulted has so obviously been to their great misfortune that no further comment need be expended upon the matter.

Not all is lost, however. For during the millennia certain individuals among these lowly evolved Antipodeans spent among the civilised created in Europe, something of the religious impulse must have penetrated their primitive psyches. This same religious impulse is now, slowly, rising to the surface and finding expression in a wonderful attitude denoted 'saviourism'. Of course, Neanderthal-like as they are in these matters, Antipodeans do not have faith in that supreme figure, that saviour among saviours, Jesus Christ. No. Antipodeans are much coarser in their appreciation both of the sorrow of their situation and of the one who is available to save them from it.

Naively, they believe they were born to enjoy themselves to the utmost. A saviour worthy of worship is anyone who leads them towards such a state. Accordingly sportsmen, movie stars, entertainers, politicians, pop singers, controversy-starters, personalities – all, at various times, wear the mantle of 'saviour'.

No doubt this desire for a saviour is deeply rooted in the Antipodean psyche, for just as the civilised were given a comforter by their saviour – otherwise known as the Holy Spirit – so do Antipodeans have a comforter of their own, given to them by their saviours, a comforter which may be called 'the pleasure principle'. The chief impetus of this principle is self-explanatory, but the nature of its manifestation is worth briefly considering.

That Christmas is the most important date on the Christian calendar is a fact that requires no verification. It is a time in which food and drink are ingested for the expanded benevolence of the body spiritual, gifts are exchanged, harmony and love (the twin thrusts of the Christian message) are endemic, and the glory which is Christianity is seen in all its haloed wonder. A blessed time it is – which has immediately become subverted by the pleasure principle. Thus the greatest of spiritual events is, in Antipodean hands, merely another excuse for immodest behaviour. This means that whenever Antipodeans indulge in various delights, they refer to the experience as 'being Christmas'. Not only that, but their ideal is that every day should be this very same 'Christmas'. And their perpetual hope is that 'all their Christmases should come at once.'

Every successful festival depends on the generosity of those involved. Antipodean generosity, in seeking to make life perpetually 'Christmas', involves such felicitous contributions as attempting to have their Christmas pud and eat it too; for Antipodean males, keeping a sharp eye out for virgins; and in partaking of Christ's blood as frequently as possible (and not always in the form of consecrated wine: how the host ends up under the table we will ignore).

Such spiritual aberrations naturally send shudders through the souls of the devout. One can only pray that a return will be made and that religious practices as maintained in civilised lands by created peoples will one day reach the Antipodes. There is no doubt that an Inquisition or two, a large number of Papal Bulls, and excommunication of large numbers of the evolved, would have a sobering effect on Antipodean attitudes.

Yet do not despair, you among the devout, at contemplating the Antipodean ape. The agencies of religion, long experienced in these matters, and in dealing with the heathen element, realised that a stabilising influence needed to be applied to the Antipodean psyche. Accordingly, when the first colonial ships arrived at these shores ministers of the cloth disembarked among the colonisers. These fine ministers took quick stock of the situation and immediately set about making the necessary corrections.

What they found was that a certain native race, the Māori, had preceded the arrival of tree-seeking colonialists by several centuries, and had established their own way of life in these tree festooned isles. One of the chief characteristics exhibited by the Māori was an attachment to their possessions, especially to their families, homes, land and skins.

Observing this attachment, and knowing attachments stop believers from reaching the place all Christians seek – that a rich man cannot enter heaven – these worthy ministers did what any concerned religious would do in order to save the heathen soul: they actively campaigned to take those families, homes, land and skin from the benighted Māori and thus enable them, poorer but infinitely freer, to enter the Great Abode Above.

That, of course, left the small problem of what to do with the homes and lands. A difficult problem, much contemplated. And finally resolved. For being the self-sacrificing people men of the cloth are all around the world, the clergy decided to accept the burden of those material possessions on themselves, sacrificing their own soulful futures that the (now poorer) natives may have the opportunity of inheriting an eternity of bliss. Truly, they are a light which shines down even to these troubled times!

However, clerical concern wasn't the only force that entered the lives of these 'ignorant' natives. Among the debased evolved line of those who sought a new life among Antipodean trees were a small number whose spiritual intuition was evidently finely tuned to the will of the Lord. These sensitives having, no doubt, obtained Word From Above, decided that they too should share their vision of a blissful eternity with the aforementioned natives. Hence they decided not only to describe the horrors of hell which befall those who exclude themselves from the Lord's grace, but to literally re-create in graphic detail on Earth a reflection of what an afterlife in fire and brimstone must be.

Thus numbers of them went out and set fire to Māori homes, spread death and destruction, caused much gnashing of teeth, and generally 'gave them hell'. The Māori proved to be of great spiritual capacity, however, and realising that all good Christians should exhibit missionary zeal, and wanting very much to be good Christians, they 'gave hell' back to the tree-loving colonialists. Unfortunately, the crown misinterpreted events and sent in soldiers who killed off large numbers of them. Yet mysterious are the ways of the Lord. For perhaps they will all be Up There waiting for the very few of us who will eventually join them.

But enough of past and present. What may be said of the likely future trend in the Antipodes as regards the wonderful civilising influence of religion?

Perhaps the best way to answer this question is to pass beyond Antipodean boundaries and look at the possible future not merely in terms partisan to the Antipodes, but as regards the future of the planet as a whole. Looking thus, what do we see?

First, that the planet is far more Christianised than people generally think. That the two mightiest powers, the USA and the USSR, have opposed political ideologies is well known, but that they are both Christian nations, not just the former, is not so widely appreciated. Why, you ask? The answer is straightforward.

Christ arrived to alleviate us poor human beings of our burdens of sin. Everyone is familiar with this doctrine. Furthermore, Christ will return to establish paradise on Earth. Wonderful. Everyone wants to live in paradise. Even communists. This paradise on Earth has an official title, spoken of in a certain manner when communication is made with Those Above. The title? Kingdom Come. This very same Kingdom Come is the goal which animates good Christian endeavor, both in terms of preparing the faithful for its arrival and in establishing in others a similar desire.

And here is where the American and Soviet attitudes display a like-minded Christian zeal. Who said nuclear weapons are a negative presence? Out of spiritual consideration for one and all, both superpowers wish to blow us to Kingdom Come as quickly as can be arranged. If they succeed, what wonder. Then we would be able to affirm, Antipodeans and civilised alike, that indeed, contrary to expectations, all our Christmases *had* come at once. And what may that give rise to but a sigh of complete and utter bliss?

On Ascension to Paradise

> Ascension to paradise depends on the acolyte having in his or her possession a certain pie. Without this pie, the acolyte's hopes of ascension are mere dreams and fancies; but with this pie inconceivable joys and ecstasies follow automatically, and he or she is initiated into all which is supernal and divine. Therefore, if you would reach paradise, seek out this pie. Possess it and digest it. That is the only way by which you will ever fulfil yourself and discover the goal of all human longing.

The above quotation is extracted from an unpublished collection written by a contemplative who wishes to remain anonymous. His essays are full of elusive allusions and subtle arguments felicitous to God's design, and as such are the food of the few who are tuned to fine sentiments; the many, lacking the stomach for higher thoughts, are excluded because lofty advice would only confuse them further. Fearing this confusion, the divine who wrote this paragraph has previously eschewed publication. But having played upon his desire to illuminate humanity's dark heart, we have persuaded him to allow the inclusion here of his admonishment on the connectedness of paradise to the tasting of pies.

Do we detect a smile on our reader's lips? Laugh if you wish. But know you are showing you are one of the unripe who, because of their coarseness, find the truly spiritual passes them by. The divine feared just this ridicule, and so his hesitation regarding publication. But we persuaded him that we would explain to the coarse exactly what is meant by these extraordinary words. Therefore, doubters, let us expound the subtleties you laugh at. Listen and learn.

Pies bear upon our lives with great intimacy. Naturally, this is not immediately obvious, especially if it is argued that many people partake of pies irregularly, or even not at all. But rest easy.

Of course, we are not speaking literally. How, then, do we speak? Allegorically. Hence, the word 'pie' allegorically represents all that the human appetite partakes of, whether that be meat, vegetable, bread, cake, or any other delicacy.

To extend the allegory. That familiarity breeds contempt is a well-known and well-documented observation of human activities. What this homily implies is that the human heart naturally seeks escape from mundane and repetitive experiences of everyday existence by chasing the unfamiliar, the mysterious, the enticing. Thus we see people eager to travel, to visit exotic places, to meet new and important people, to have intoxicating experiences – all of which are symptoms of the need to escape the mundane. Naturally, what is true of humankind's impulses generally is true of allegorical 'pies' in particular. Accordingly, we see that many people, tired of their ordinary everyday cooking, line up at pie-shops in order to experience the 'extraordinary'. This tendency we could speak of as the desire 'to have it with cream'. No matter what the experience, as human beings we want the best, the most intoxicating, the most delicious – in short, we want to 'have it with cream'. Again, the allegorical 'pie' which is the subject of this exegesis does not lack in this particular. Hence, it too is trimmed with an allegorical 'cream' – 'cream' being the joy and ecstasy which is the soul's sustenance. Get your 'laughing gear' into that!

Yet while we have explicated the 'pie' and 'cream' in so far as their general allegorical meaning is concerned, we have yet to explicate 'pie' as regards its fundamental and universal form.

For the 'pie' exists on not only the literal and allegorical levels. It also exists as a spiritual entity in its own right, transcending this world and all who live in it. And it is here that our anonymous divine presents his coup d'etat. It is here that his profound subtlety becomes apparent. What is the nature of this 'pie' that makes it so remarkable? It is nothing short of ..... the-pie-in-the-sky. No allegorical being this. Wrap your 'laughing gear' around it. And make sure you 'have it with cream'! For the pie-in-the-sky is the greatest, most unforgettable experience available in the emporium of human possibilities.

Happily, all will now comprehend something of the depth of intuitive understanding which is expressed in the few words which head this exposition. Yet we have still merely glanced at its wisdom. We leave readers to plunge, at their leisure, into its very depths.

But, before we finish, one more point should be made. A point which, while not explicitly stated in the original sermon, is implied by it, and is thus a necessary corollary of its central truth. Specifically, this is in reference to the word 'pied'. Generally, 'pied' is used to describe something which has a mottled, multicoloured appearance. This is the meaning when the Pied Piper is usually spoken of: he was a piper who wore clothing of many colours, and thus is 'pied'. However, there is an alternative, spiritual level of meaning to the story of the Pied Piper. For a tradition exists among the few that once one has reached and partaken of the-pie-in-the-sky, one becomes an initiate. And just as one who loses his possessions becomes 'dispossessed', and one who gains a knighthood becomes 'knighted', so one who partakes of the-pie-in-the-sky becomes 'pied'. Such is the secret meaning of the 'Pied' Piper. He was one of the few who tasted the-pie-in-the-sky. And having tasted it, he wished to share it. Accordingly, in his musical activities he sought to rid the coarse of the 'rats' which infest the human heart and to lead the children of Earth into the heavenly kingdom of 'pie-in-the-sky'. Moreover, as shown by the intoxicating power of his music, he sought 'to dish it out with cream'.

Of course, this is still far from a full exposition of our divine's words. One obvious question that arises from the preceding is what is meant when someone is described as 'pie-eyed'. Great truths reside in this term. However, this is as far as we are authorised to proceed at this time. Those whose hearts and minds thirst for the deepest truths must wait the arrival of another, more deeply versed in spiritual insights than we.

Psyche, Metaphysics and the Meaning of Life

To the sophisticated reader, the primitive state of life in the Antipodes will be appalling. How, in the twentieth century, could there exist human beings (if Antipodeans, for the reasons previously discussed, can be regarded as human beings) whose perception of reality is so askew? Clearly, in the greater centres of civilisation no such aberration of attitude occurs. There all function in harmony with the highest liberal impulses: compassion, generosity, willingness to share, a propensity to think before acting, and a deep regard for consequences, no matter how small the action. Unfortunately, no such impulses animate the Antipodean b(r)east. Indeed, the cultured have yet to hear the worst.

Among Antipodeans there is a strong feeling, an unvanquishable feeling, that Antipodeans are different from all other human races on the planet. And not merely different. Better. S-u-p-e-r-i-o-r. Further, they not only consider themselves superior to people from non-Antipodean cultures, but they engage in intense repression of any who look or live differently from themselves. Of course, persecution per se is long established in the centres of civilisation, and is entirely reasonable behaviour. No, what disturbs about Antipodeans is not that they spurn non-Antipodeans, but that they also look down on all those who live in regions of the Antipodes other than their own. These fellow Antipodeans they abuse and vilify every opportunity they get.

Yet that is still not the end of Antipodean social gymnastics. For, despite the friction that grinds constantly between the many Antipodean regional groups, whenever Antipodeans are threatened by outsiders they all forget past divisions and immediately join into a single identity to repulse the intruder. This process they, in their wisdom, call 'patriotism'.

The concept of patriotism is very interesting, indicative as it is of much which lurks in the shadows of the Antipodean psyche. The Greeks, as we all know, defined 'psyche' as breath, the soul, the life-force. Young children often practise holding their breath for as long as they can. The primitives who live in the Antipodes are still holding theirs. Thus we see that numerous extruded manifestations of the psyche – social dysfunction, psychosis, psychopathy – are alive and well in these blessed isles. With, in the case of patriotism, a fair dose of schizophrenia thrown in for good measure.

A view exists among the informed that our forebears once existed in a Golden Age, living a gentle, wise, compassionate life, harmonious with the Powers Above and tender towards all living beings. Today many consider that the Antipodes (primitive though all agree it is) is the one land where remnants of the Golden Age may still be observed. Many Antipodeans themselves believe in and encourage this view, calling their land Godzone, and promoting a picture of themselves as 'nature's innocent children'. In fact, they have a saying which sums up their childlike enjoyment of such Golden Age activities as physical movement, the engagement of the senses, and the thrill of frolicking and tumbling. A saying which enthusiastically pronounces, 'If it's down, kick it'.

Which brings us to another observation regarding the Antipodean psyche. For no matter how long one dawdles in the back alleys of sociological and anthropological investigation, one must finally enter the main street of human activity and confront the one question beside which all others pale into insignificance. Namely: What animates the Antipodean? What fundamental impulse drives the Antipodean to climb out of bed in the morning and engage with the day? In a word, what makes the Antipodean live?

Immediately, a further thought comes to mind: Is what Antipodeans do really living? Many wonder if there is life after death. Fewer question the assumption that there is life before death. The answer is not so obvious, if one takes into consideration the action of the previously-mentioned patriotism. A well-known behaviourist once postulated a black box theory to describe human psychology: input stimuli, and out comes pre-programmed behaviour. The case of patriotism validates this model: put in a threat to national pride, and out comes the language of vilification and postures of aggression. Given that the black box model is mechanical and automatic in process, and given further that mechanical systems are not considered to be alive, one is left questioning the assumption that there is human life in the Antipodes. But we have again wandered from the central thrust of our investigation.

A description of the purpose of Antipodean life (assuming, for the sake of argument, that such life exists) must now be attempted. Where to start? Perhaps we should first ask the typical Antipodean how he or she views the purpose of his or her own life. This we did by going out into streets and shopping malls and randomly questioning passers-by. The answer? Overwhelmingly, they answered: To bring others into the world that they may 'carry on'. This is to be expected. Indeed, even that great source of wisdom says as much, quoting the Lord as saying, 'Go forth and multiply.' (That Paul came along later and said, 'Multiply, yes, but don't enjoy it,' is another matter.)

But, the perspicacious reader will be objecting at this point, cats and dogs multiply. How do Antipodeans differ from these? An excellent question. Easily answered. For cats and dogs cannot be referred to in the same breath as Antipodeans. Why? Because cats and dogs don't think. Whereas Antipodeans do. (Granted, this last assertion has little basis in fact, but if we regard it as being a potential which may, at any moment, come into reality, we will be able to carry on in good faith.) Accepting then that Antipodeans do, or may, at some unspecified future date, start to, think, the next question logically arises: What do Antipodeans think about? Do they, dare one ask, think about the purpose of life? And, if they do, what do they conclude?

Thus far we have been at pains to delineate the manner in which the Antipodean psyche differs from that of civilised peoples. But, in fact, this is one instance where Antipodeans adhere to the norm. For as soon as they are asked about life and its purpose, the last issue they wish to consider is death. Indeed, death is a topic which is avoided in all polite company, Antipodean or civilised. But it must be asked because it leads to the deepest aspect of this question: In the face of death, what is the purpose of life? What is the point in living, struggling, fighting to establish a better life, if death is going to nullify everything that is achieved? In the face of death, does life still have a purpose? And if so, what is it?

This is a question of profound philosophic import. Which requires the application of philosophic skills. Socrates, midwife to philosophic thought, perfected the art of arguing from analogy. Thus we too should create an analogous situation and ask a question of it, that illumination may be cast, by reflection, on what we really want to know. Accordingly, by way of analogy, we may pertinently ask: How far should one go on a first date?

No, do not laugh. Such an analogy is not as far-fetched as it seems. For when one considers the matter deeply, it becomes apparent that there are three basic actions available. The first is that of quitting after the initial attempt; the second is going far enough to stimulate the desire for a second date; and the third is whole hog. Similar attitudes may be adopted with regard to life and death. Some believe in playing safe; others take the occasional chance, skating around the edge of risk but with only the very faintest possibility of falling in; while others throw caution to the winds and commit body, heart, mind and soul. Such a range of responses may also be discerned among Antipodeans. For there exists a 'certain something', the presence or absence of which demarcates whether one is living with or without risk. This 'certain something' is of enormous social, psychological, philosophic, aesthetic and spiritual significance. It lies at the heart of Antipodean society; without it there is great doubt as to whether, in fact, one lives at all. What is this 'certain something'? It is described in two words: Credit card.

This is the 'certain something' which allows Antipodeans to weld their own interpretation of the ancient religious concepts, 'saved', and 'we will all be called to account'. During the passage of the past several centuries, science – whether occult or secular

– has worked to achieve the triumph of mind over matter. The Antipodes is a wonderful working example of the triumph of matter over mind. And so it is, finally, that we arrive at the answer to our question regarding what Antipodeans think regarding the purpose of life. For the truth is that Antipodeans do not have a clue.

Yet we should not end on a querulous note. Because if Antipodeans lack a metaphysical purpose, this is clearly not the case in the greater centres of contemporary civilisation. There ideal models of social and religious behaviour have long been the substance of everyday life, animating every human being, enabling all to live a rich and generous existence. This being the case, we empty Antipodeans should pause a moment and regard these superior beings. What guides the civilised? What impulse gives them their purpose?

The answer is clear and unequivocal. The civilised have for centuries had among them many of the greatest religious and philosophic thinkers who have yet lived. How does their influence manifest? In the ways current inhabitants of the greater centres of civilisation show themselves to be conscience-driven, humane, understanding, sympathetic, supportive and generous.

For although Antipodeans do not realise it, trapped as they are within the borders of their own narrow concerns, in many countries around the world not only is death thought of a great deal, but their citizens have the opportunity to daily test their philosophic outlook in the face of it. Well aware of this, the civilised cannot but obey the drive of their consciences and so engage in helping those unfortunates escape ignorance, disease, poverty, exploitation, starvation, illiteracy, war and numerous other ills.

To do so, the civilised apply the profound religious principles of faith, hope and charity. This is witnessed by their unwavering hope of building weak nations into strong, their vast faith that such shall inevitably come about, and their bottomless charity in helping the undeveloped achieve this goal. To illustrate how selflessnessly they apply their deeply felt principles around the globe, we choose instances at random.

There is the assistance given Brazil to rid itself of its pesky rain forests, so unsightly and wild, and the sending of missionaries to help the unfortunate natives lost so deep in those forests that for tens of thousands of years they have had no choice but to live in harmony with nature. There is the support given Chile to extract copper from its mountains, including providing the military with the training necessary for a stable regime to be established, thus ensuring the wider populace has no doubts as to its future. There is the aid offered to India when clouds of poisonous gas exploded from a local factory, with international companies helping them re-establish manufacturing processes harmonious with standards set in the boardrooms of the civilised. And, finally, there is the aid given the Indonesians in their innovative quest to establish a game park in East Timor, complete with turkey shoots in which, and this is a heart-warming touch, even the Australian media are encouraged to take part.

Antipodeans are frequently, and justly, accused of not aiding the less fortunate in the way the civilised so generously do. Truly, those civilized are the models. We, wrapped in the flax ropes of primitive illusions, can only watch admiringly, knowing we have so much to learn, such an immense moral distance to travel.

Afterword

Literary tradition demands that before we send this work to the publisher a note from the author appendise the preceding and bring the whole to a decisive end. Having reached that place now, we find ourselves obliged to produce this afterword. One difficulty complicates this task, however. It is that we have nothing left to say.

This is a dilemma many authors face at some stage of their careers, the devouring chasm that must be struggled across. We are only prevented from despairing utterly by the knowledge that some ingenious authors have dealt with this dilemma so successfully that they have built entire careers on it. We do not find ourselves of their number. Despite the enormous invention leaking from the preceding pages, the reader now finds us dried of inspiration, lacking any notion of how to compose the final flourish which an effort otherwise so resourceful demands.

Indeed, we admit some time has been spent staring at the keyboard, at the wall, and at shelves full of fecund volumes almost audibly laughing at us as we attempted to wring a last incandescent paragraph from our dried brain. Nothing arrived. Then ... a matterphysical realisation!

This realisation is that, despite the impressive erudition of the preceding pages, our work lacks a last impression which will leave the reader in absolutely no doubt that we belong in the drawing room of literary aristocracy, that our aspirations are not merely noble, but Nobel, in scope. Further, this impression may only be effected via a quotation that is simultaneously profound, witty, solemn, flashy, insightful, accessible, familiar and obscure.

By this we mean that we require a final quotation that is sufficiently well known that reviewers may recognise it, yet not so widely known that the nose-dripping hoi polloi may recognise it too. After all, the whole point of parading learning is to repeat something that is sufficiently part of the literary lexicon that the initiated will recognise it and applaud the one who quotes it, but is sufficiently unknown that one's aunt visiting from the sticks is in no position to assert, 'Oh, I knew *that*!'

Yet this is not all. The issue is complicated by one further factor: the illiteracy phenomenon. This is the circumstance whereby one knows that an author has entered the pantheon because everyone has heard of their work, recognises the odd title, can perhaps quote a line or two (maybe even accurately), but – and here is the rub – today no one reads them. We know such authors are haloed because, and here we borrow from one of the pantheon, great literature is 'a custom more honoured in the breach than the observance'.

But perhaps we are making a mistake. For undoubtedly all our reviewers will recognise the source of this phrase. Yet few will feel confident they should show their learning by referencing it, given it is likely many of the cultured readers they write for will respond, 'Oh, I knew *that*!' From the perspective of seeking a review that toasts our talents to the east and west, that uncertainty will certainly not elevate us into even the lower ranks of literary stars. Thankfully, however, the above quotation is not the final flourish with which we are disposed to conclude this work.

Rather, we have decided to end by quoting an author of whom everyone undoubtedly has heard, but whose work only a hyper-literate few (besides an undergraduate working under compulsion) would think of reading today. Yet this author has such a ready wit that, whether or not the quotation is recognised, the reader cannot but appreciate its aptness to the present work. Therefore, dear reader, please welcome that most luminous of literary superstars, Mr Jonathan Swift:

> I am now trying an Experiment very frequent among Modern Authors; which is, to write upon Nothing; When the subject is utterly exhausted, to let the Pen still move on; by some called the Ghost of Wit, delighting to walk after the Death of the Body. And to

say the Truth, there seems to be no part of Knowledge in fewer hands, than That of Discerning when to have Done. By the Time that an Author has writ out a Book, he and his Readers are become old Acquaintances, and grow very loath to part: So that I have sometimes known it in Writing, as in Visiting, where the Ceremony of taking Leave has employ'd more Time than the whole Conversation before.

Having noted which, we too, not wishing to outlast our good reader's patience, make a discreet but decisive bolt for the door.

Jerusalem, 52 CE ____ [1986–1989]

Paul addresses the people of Jerusalem

The Acts According to Luke records that Paul of Tarsus and his companions entered Jerusalem's Temple to perform purification rituals. Their intent is recorded as being to put to rest doubts regarding Paul's orthodoxy with respect to Jewish religious practices. However, in the Temple he was recognised by some who roused worshippers against him by claiming he preached against their religious doctrines and laws, and that he had profaned the Temple by bringing a Greek into its precincts. Neither claim was true. Nonetheless, a riot ensued, Paul was seized, and only the arrival of Roman solders stopped him from being killed. The soldiers decided to take Paul to the fortress for his own safety. As they approached the fortress Paul asked the centurion in charge if he could address the following crowd. He was granted permission, and waved the crowd to silence.

> When all was quiet again he spoke to them
> in Hebrew. – Acts 21:40

My fathers, my brothers, hear my defence.
Though born in Tarsus I am, like you, a Jew,
raised by an uncle here in Jerusalem,
versed in the Holy Law by Gamaliel,
a rabbi whose piety and learning
are famed among the gentiles even,
from Alexandria to the Western Isles.
No student of Gamaliel's school lacks
teaching in the Law's exact observance,
and I proved myself a worthy student.
In fact, I strode so faithfully the path

our ancestors laid by our God's strict command,
so perfectly followed Pharisee practice
in all its patterns and complexities,
I formed a living mirror to the Law,
as duteous to the Lord's will as those
who sought, in the Temple, to stone me today.
So perfect was my duty to our God,
so ardent my desire to prove his champion,
I sent scores of heretics to prison.
So purely I loved my ancestors' God,
and yours, Lord Yahweh Sabaoth!
If any here doubt my integrity,
question Jonathan, or the Sanhedrin.
For them, to their brothers in Damascus,
I carried letters and encouragement,
intent to return with prisoners
for punishment here in Jerusalem.
But on that journey, outside Damascus' walls,
a holy spectre transformed my mission.
I saw, from the heavens, a fire descend,
the like of which no man before has seen,
except perhaps Moses, surprised by leaves
burning on the lonely peak of Sinai.
An unearthly fire, of flames that leapt
but did not consume, it filled the entire world,
ground to sky, with light so terrible
and holy it struck me blinded from my mule.
Yet as I lay there, chest heaving, groping
a bloodied hand through the dust for my staff,
the Lord's gracious spirit entered my soul
and revelation transported me to
where few since the earliest days have been,
when prophecy strode Judaea naked,
and Yacob climbed his ladder to heaven.

I saw, ranged before me, with sight not bodily
but wholly inward, Yahweh's great glory.
Words cannot describe the divine presence:
enough that my joyful soul ignited
and I was lost, consumed by ecstatic flame.
Three days passed till I returned to this world,
my soul's direction forever altered.
And with it came a new understanding.
I saw the Law won't take us to Yahweh.
Less: it keeps us from the holy presence.
Feasting and fasting, sacrifice and prayer,
all the long-prescribed rituals of our tribes
which hang so heavy with social command
and weave the fabric of our daily life,
these are as nothing on the path to heaven.
Brothers, hear me. To practise the Law is good.
But we practise the Law to reach Yahweh,
and Yahweh resides far beyond the Law.
So don't make the Law a false god, worshipping
which keeps you from the goodness of heaven.

Paul addresses the Sanhedrin

The next day, the tribune wanted to know what
precise charges the Jews were bringing, so he
freed Paul and gave orders for a meeting of the
chief priests and all the Sanhedrin. – Acts 22:31

Brothers, I greet you. Fourteen years have passed
since last I was in Jerusalem, yet
I see by your eyes I am not forgotten.
Abubas, Jehial, Hebron, you others
I recognise but cannot name, shalom.
I am a Pharisee and a Pharisee's son,
born to traditions as much a part of me
as this land, these legs I stand on. No, more.
Cut off my hand, I am who I am still,
but remove my birthright and I am nothing.
In this I am, like you, a child of my time,
helpless to our forefathers' covenants,
traditions from which I have never departed.
This the Sanhedrin itself recognises,
for it has, in the past, used my wisdom
to implement its chosen policies.
I was efficient and obedient.
I persecuted the Law against heresies
of all kinds, and was applauded for such
right here, in this room, by this selfsame body.
So why then, if my worth is acknowledged,
am I arraigned before you all today?
My brothers, I stand before you unsubdued,
because to this very moment I can swear,
in here, on the touchstone of my conscience,
that I have never, in any action,

broken a single of Yahweh's commands.
Our Lord said: Worship no god beside me.
You wish to try me according to the Law.
The Law's purpose is to ensure we live
harmonious to Yahweh's will and covenant,
that by remembering Him, He'll remember us.
Yet, brothers, are we remembering Yahweh
when we persecute the Law to its limits?
Or is our love for the Law and its processes
holding us from Yahweh and his wisdom;
are we making of the Law an idol,
the which we worship at Yahweh's expense?
Know I have never strayed from Yahweh's path;
rather I have walked it farther than you.
Our God is a living god, confined to
neither flesh nor word: He halts the waters,
speaks from whirlwinds, appears as fire,
lowers ladders from heaven He calls us to climb.
His angels were created to guide us,
His dark judgement to lovingly chastise us,
His power to administer all the world;
yet when the blind worm cries, He knows, He is there.
Hold a thought, it has already been thought;
draw a breath and it is breathed. Nothing is
but as He wills it: His holy presence
fills everything we think, say, or do.
This, brothers, is the living power
by which we may worship our living God,
a power which makes the living to die,
yet chooses also to resurrect those dead.
I am not here for betraying the Law:
none has, or can, put evidence that I have.
But many here hate me. Why? Brothers, listen.
It's Sadducee voices that bay for my head,

because I am true to my Pharisee fathers,
and teach the ignorant of Yahweh's
merciful power to resurrect the dead!

Paul answers the Roman governor

Five days later the high priest Ananias came down
with some of the elders and an advocate named
Tertullus, and they laid information against Paul
before the governor, Felix Antonius. – Acts 24:1

Excellency, I know Rome loves justice,
so I will not fear to speak the truth.
As is easily verified, I have been
in Jerusalem no longer than twelve days.
I came here on a pilgrimage, to worship
my fathers' God in His holy temple.
That was all my purpose in visiting,
which the high priest and the rest well know,
for I am loyal to the same God as they.
Once in the temple I was mistaken
by the crowd for another, from whose wrath
the tribune and his soldiers extracted me.
This is the full reason for my being here.
Plainly, there is no case to answer.
Rather, consider this: I am here today
because I accept the truth of resurrection.
Some here would ask how dead corpses are raised,
and what manner of body they would wear.
Are the bones reknitted together? Does what
the worms have eaten reconstitute itself?
Clearly, physical resurrection is absurd:
neither do I accept such foolishness.
What is sown in the ground has first to die
before it is given new life, while what
you sow is not what is going to come.
Plant wheat and the seed dies that the body

God has chosen may come into being;
plant barley, corn or jute and each seed type
manifests its own particular body.
This same principle equally applies
when we consider the resurrection:
what is sown is perishable, but what
is resurrected is imperishable;
what is sown is a physical body,
what is raised is spiritual utterly.
For neither flesh inherits God's kingdom,
nor does the perishable inherit eternity.
Rather, when the physical body suffers death
our inward spirit, safely encased in
its resurrection body, will survive
to wander those realms of which we know little,
yet provide our place of dwelling after death.
I know this sounds strange, but when did strangeness
justify the Sanhedrin's call for my death?
For that will surely be its lawful judgement.
But I am a citizen of Rome, standing
before Caesar's appointed tribunal;
here, and here only, is where I should be tried.
If I am guilty of any capital crime
let me not to escape the death penalty.
But if these accusations lack substance,
none, not even you Antonius Felix,
has the right to surrender me to them.
Thus, as is my right, I appeal to Caesar.

Paul addresses visitors to his cell

Brothers, sisters, last night I had a dream.
I dreamed I saw a man of wisdom who,
fourteen long years past, I do not know how,
the Lord lifted to the highest heavens.
Such mysteries he witnessed, such secrets heard,
that no human tongue is able to describe.
Yet this he proclaimed: from God's pleroma,
where stands light-world upon light-world, and vast
aeon powers in hierarchy arrayed,
from this perfection, in love and wisdom,
our Lord God has sent down to Earth a power
so subtle, yet so all-transforming, that
whoever it touches shall not remain unchanged.
This is Chrestos, his light-power supreme,
first-born of his loving compassion,
whereby our hidden selves are fed and sustained.
To this then I pray, kneeling before you,
and to our father Yahweh, who guides us all:
Lord, redeem our eternal spirits from death;
reveal the first-born of your grace to our minds;
grant us, your children, what no angel eye has seen,
angel ear heard, nor has entered the human heart;
what in the beginning was formed in the image
of the incorruptible psychic God.
And place on us your elect and beloved greatness,
the first-begotten mystery of your house,
since in you we have placed our faith and hope.
For yours is the power, the blessing and glory,
for ever and ever. Amen.

A Brief History of the World, Part 2 _____ [1984 / 1990]

The Fall

CHARACTERS

ADAM
EVE
CAIN
ABEL
SNAKE
PROPHET

SETTING

The action takes place on a minimally lit bare stage. The acting may use props or mime, or a combination.

NOTES ON CHARACTERS

ADAM, EVE, CAIN and ABEL move like string puppets; that is, as if they had strings attached to their hands, arms, feet, legs, and head, the controlling ends of which are held by some unseen being positioned directly above the stage.

The stage direction, 'Cry out loud' is a sharp 'Waaaah!', which begins abruptly, ends abruptly, and lasts only a short time. There should be no sobbing nor any attempt to sound anguished, hurt or emotional.

Lights up.

ADAM rolls onto the stage.

Pause.

ADAM stands, takes up the attitude of a string puppet.

Walks jerkily.

Stops.

Looks at his feet.

Looks at his hands.

Looks above.

Looks at the audience.

Cries out loud.

EVE rolls onto the stage.

ADAM stops crying out loud.

EVE stands, takes up the attitude of a string puppet.

Looks at her feet.

Looks at her hands.

Looks at ADAM, who is looking at her.

Both cry out loud.

A tree descends, settles on the stage.

Both stop crying out loud.

ADAM and EVE look at the tree.

An apple is attached to one of the branches.

Look at each other.

Look at the tree.

Simultaneously, both approach the tree.

A sign descends from above, hovers over the tree. It says:

DON'T TOUCH.

Both look at the sign.

Look above.

Look at the apple.

Look at each other.

Simultaneously, they reach out towards the apple.

A growl from above.

They are jerked away by pulls on their strings.

They come to a rest on opposite wings of the stage.

They look at each other.

Look above.

Look at the audience.

Pause.

A SNAKE appears between the branches of the tree.

Hisses.

ADAM and EVE turn to look at it.

EVE approaches the tree, pulls off the apple, examines it.

She holds it out to ADAM.

ADAM approaches.

Looks at the apple.

Both look above.

Look at the SNAKE.

Look at each other.

Pause.

Simultaneously, ADAM and EVE lean forwards and take a bite from the apple.

Chew, swallow.

They look at each other.

The SNAKE looks from EVE to ADAM.

Simultaneously, ADAM and EVE cry aloud.

A roar, above.

ADAM and EVE huddle together.

The SNAKE exits.

The tree is lifted above.

The roar dies.

Pause.

They look up.

Look at the audience.

Two bassinets roll squeakily on-stage, from either wing.

ADAM and EVE straighten, look at the bassinets.

The bassinets halt.

ADAM and EVE each apporach a bassinet.

Look inside.

Look at each other.

Pause.

A sign descends, hovers over the bassinets: PROCREATE.

ADAM and EVE are jerked towards each other.

Their efforts to stop their movement is fruitless.

They end in the centre of the stage, face to face.

A growl from above.

ADAM and EVE put their arms around each other.

EVE's stomach immediately swells up, forcing ADAM back.

EVE crouches.

Her stomach goes down.

Crying out loud sounds from both bassinets.

ADAM and EVE approach the bassinets.

Look into them.

Look above.

Look at each other.

Cry out loud.

Pause.

The card, which says, PROCREATE jiggles.

ADAM and EVE look at the sign.

Look at the bassinets.

Look at each other.

EVE's hands move without her volition, take both her breasts, squeeze them.

Streams of milk fly through the air from her breasts into the bassinets.

The crying stops.

EVE'S hands stop squeezing, the milk stops flying.

EVE'S hands release the breasts.

ADAM and EVE relax.

Pause.

A box descends from above. Settles on the stage.

A card descends, hovers over the box. It says: WORK.

ADAM and EVE look at the card.

Look at the box.

Look at each other.

Pause.

A growl from above.

ADAM and EVE are jerked towards the box, halt beside it, look down.

The sides fall, revealing a spade, a watering can and a small box.

The card that says WORK jiggles.

ADAM picks up the shovel, digs a hole.

EVE picks up the small box, places the box in the hole.

ADAM picks up the watering can, pours it over the box.

Nothing happens.

ADAM tips the can upside down: it is empty.

ADAM and EVE look at the watering can.

Look at each other.

Simultaneously, they bend over the can, cry out loud.

ADAM pours it over the small box.

A tree shoots out of the small box, grows rapidly.

Fruit hangs on it.

ADAM and EVE each pick a piece of fruit.

Eat.

Crying out loud from the bassinets.

ADAM and EVE stop eating.

Look at each other.

Look at the bassinets.

Look at the fruit.

Walk over.

Put the fruit into each of the bassinets.

The crying stops.

ADAM and EVE relax.

A card descends, hovers over the stage: WORSHIP.

Look above.

Look at the audience.

ADAM and EVE look at each other.

Simultaneously, they utter hymn-like noises.

Roses fall from above.

ADAM and EVE stop singing.

They pick up the roses, are pricked by thorns.

Both cry out loud.

Throw the roses down.

Look at the roses.

Look above.

Look at each other.

Pick up the roses.

Each drops a rose into a bassinet.

ADAM and EVE take up postures of repose.

Pause.

The bassinets wheel slowly off-stage.

As the first disappears, CAIN appears and takes its place.

As the second disappears, ABEL appears and takes its place.

CAIN and ABEL are jerked to centre stage.

ABEL smiles.

CAIN blows out of his mouth a large number of rose petals.

A card descends, hovers over CAIN and ABEL: TEACH.

ADAM and EVE look at the card.

Look above.

Look at CAIN and ABEL

Look at each other.

Simultaneously, they step forwards.

Slap CAIN and ABEL.

CAIN and ABEL cry out loud.

Pause.

Fanfare, above.

An explosion of smoke.

PROPHET, wearing wings and carrying a slate, appears.

PROPHET in turn looks at each of the four.

PROPHET clears his throat.

The four watch.

PROPHET continues clearing his throat.

The four wait.

PROPHET raises the slate.

PROPHET completes clearing his throat.

PROPHET looks at each in turn.

Raises the slate.

Opens his mouth to speak.

The slate slips from PROPHET'S hands.

It shatters.

Silence.

Simultaneously, ADAM, EVE, CAIN and ABEL laugh.

PROPHET'S wings fall off.

The four stop laughing.

Pause.

PROPHET looks at the wings.

Looks above.

Looks at the four.

Looks at audience.

Cries continuously out loud.

EVE steps up and slaps him.

PROPHET stops crying out loud.

Turns.

Exits.

Pause.

The sign which says WORK jiggles.

Simultaneously, the four turn their backs on it.

Pause.

A growl from above.

Abruptly, all are jerked to attention.

They begin different activities:

ADAM and EVE each lift up a wing and attempt to flap it.

CAIN picks up the spade, digs.

ABEL picks up the watering can, lifts it to water.

Nothing happens.

Pause.

ADAM and EVE drop the wings, approach ABEL.

Bend, cry out loud over the watering can, step back.

ABEL pours from the watering can.

A tree instantly sprouts.

Pause.

The card which says WORSHIP jiggles.

All four turn, look at the card.

Look above.

Look at each other.

Look at the audience.

Pause.

A growl, above.

The four are jerked around the stage.

CAIN and ABEL pick fruit off the trees.

They carry them to the front of the stage.

Put what they picked on the stage.

Stand behind their pile.

EVE and ADAM walk over, stand behind them.

Pause.

Simultaneously, all four sing with a hymn-like sound.

A beam of light is switched on above, shining onto the stage.

The light roams around the stage.

Halts on ABEL.

The four stop singing.

Pause.

CAIN looks at ABEL.

Looks above.

Looks at ADAM and EVE.

Looks at ABEL.

Steps sideways.

Places his hands on ABEL'S shoulders.

Guides ABEL to where he was standing.

Takes ABEL'S place in the light.

Pause.

The light slowly moves sideways. Halts on ABEL.

CAIN looks at ABEL.

Looks above.

Looks at ADAM and EVE.

Looks at ABEL.

Steps sideways.

Places his hands on ABEL'S shoulders.

Guides ABEL to where he was standing.

Takes ABEL'S place in the light.

Pause.

The light slowly moves sideways. Halts on ABEL.

CAIN looks at ABEL.

Looks above.

Looks at ADAM and EVE.

Looks at the audience.

CAIN picks up the spade.

Swings it above ABEL'S head, cutting his strings.

ABEL flops to the floor.

ADAM and EVE stare at ABEL.

CAIN wings the spade above EVE'S head.

Eve falls to the floor.

Swings the spade above ADAM'S head.

ADAM falls to the floor.

The three crawl on the floor.

CAIN looks up.

Swings the spade above his own head, cutting his strings.

Drops the spade.

Approaches the wings.

Picks them picks.

Stretches the out.

Stands, wings held out, flapping them slowly.

Smiles in triumph.

Hold.

CAIN collapses to the floor.

The card which says WORSHIP jiggles.

The four crawl about the stage, moaning.

The lights begin to fade.

The card which says PROCREATE jiggles.

The four crawl about the stage, moaning.

The card which says WORK jiggles.

The four crawl about the stage, moaning.

The card which says TEACH jiggles.

The four crawl about the stage, moaning.

The card which says DON'T TOUCH jiggles.

The four crawl about the stage, moaning.

The card which says WORSHIP jiggles.

The cards variously jiggle.

The four crawl about the stage, moaning.

The cards stop jiggling.

The four stop crawling.

Pause.

The cards are lifted, disappear.

The moaning dies.

Silence.

Slow fade to black.

Innerworld of the Underworld

CHARACTERS

JALAM
AARON
ELGAH
SARAH
JACOB
FIVE CREATURES
JOASH
NAOMI
ZEBAH

SETTING

The wilderness.

Blessed is the lion the man eats and the lion will become a man; and cursed is the man the lion eats and the lion will become a man. – *The Gospel According to Thomas*

Darkness.

Thunder and lightning.

Wailing human voices, off.

> VOICE 1
> (Off) Help.

> VOICE 2
> (Off) Help me.

> VOICE 3
> (Off) Help.

The calls are repeated over and over again, accompanied by random shrieks and cries of the lost and abandoned.

Lights up slowly, remaining at a low level throughout.

A howl, off.

The wailing voices become more frantic, more desperate.

Enter JALAM.

He walks slowly.

Halts centre stage.

Hold.

Enter AARON, ELGAH, SARAH, and JACOB.

They walk slowly.

They huddle together, uncertain, scared.

JALAM motions.

The voices and cries die away.

The thunder and lightning die away.

JALAM sits.

Closes his eyes.

AARON, ELGAH and SARAH stand near JALAM.

JACOB, confident, walks around.

JACOB motions.

A crack of thunder, a flash of lightning, smoke erupts from JACOB's body.

JACOB screams, falls to the floor.

The thunder and lightning continue, rise in intensity.

AARON, ELGAH and SARAH shuffle closer to JALAM.

JALAM doesn't move, eyes closed.

JACOB stands.

AARON, ELGAH and SARAH, in a huddle, face him.

JACOB runs towards one wing.

Is thrown back as if he has hit an elastic wall.

Falls to the floor.

The thunder and lightning die.

Silence.

AARON stands.

Approaches JACOB.

Prods him with a foot.

JACOB doesn't move.

A howl.

AARON rejoins the others.

Sits beside JALAM.

Howl, louder.

AARON, ELGAH and SARAH huddle closer to JALAM.

Lights fade to black.

Silence.

A scream.

Lights up.

SARAH is sitting up, facing JACOB, pointing at his body, gibbering.

ELGAH puts an arm around SARAH, who stops gibbering by degrees.

AARON stands.

Walks around the stage.

Peers into the wings.
Approaches the corpse.
Nudges it with his foot.
Approaches JALAM.
Halts in front of him.
JALAM opens his eyes.
Stands.
Walks off.
Thunder and lightning begin the moment he exits.
The wailing voices and cries start again, off.

> VOICE 1
> (Off) Help.

> VOICE 2
> (Off) Help me.

> VOICE 3
> (Off) Help.

They repeat, over and over, quickly build to a cacophony.
A howl.
AARON, ELGAH AND SARAH are buffeted by violent,
unseen forces.
JALAM enters.
Returns to the centre of the stage.
Sits.
Closes his eyes.
The screams die away.
The thunder and lightning fade.
The three are no longer buffetted.
Silence.
AARON approaches JALAM.
Sits beside him.
Closes his eyes.

The other two huddle together.

Lights slowly down.

A scream.

Lights flick up.

JACOB is on top of SARAH, choking her.

ELGAH goes to her, struggles with JACOB.

JALAM raises his hand.

A shriek, off.

JACOB goes limp.

JALAM lowers his hand.

SARAH moans.

ELGAH helps SARAH sit up.

SARAH's eyes open.

She starts to gibber.

ELGAH covers SARAH's eyes with her hand.

SARAH stops gibbering.

A howl.

JACOB sits up.

Stands.

Staggers, disorientated.

AARON opens his eyes.

Stands.

Approaches JACOB, takes him by the arm.

Sits him in front of JALAM.

Sits beside JALAM.

Closes his eyes.

Lights slowly down.

Silence.

A huge crack of thunder.

As it dies away, lights up.

AARON lies sprawled on his back.

ELGAH moves towards him.

JALAM opens his eyes.

He motions ELGAH back.

She obeys.

AARON sits up.

Turns towards JALAM.

AARON stands.

Approaches JACOB.

JACOB stands.

AARON steps towards JACOB.

JACOB backs away.

AARON takes a second step.

A third step.

JACOB turns, exits.

Rumble, off.

SARAH sits up.

ELGAH approaches her.

SARAH opens her mouth to speak.

No words come out, just a strangled croak.

JALAM stands.

AARON, ELGAH and SARAH watch.

JALAM steadies himself.

Walks slowly towards one wing as if he is wading through a thick substance.

He exits.

A growl, off.

> VOICE 1
> (Off) Help.

> VOICE 2
> (Off) Help me.

> VOICE 3
> (Off) Help.

The three voices get louder.

More demanding.

More insistent.

They abruptly cut.

AARON approaches JALAM's spot.

Sits.

Closes his eyes.

SARAH and ELGAH approach him.

Sit on either side of him.

Lights slowly down.

Silence.

A snuffling, growling sound.

SARAH whimpers.

A howl.

SARAH sobs.

A throaty, breathing sound.

SARAH cries aloud.

Lights snap up.

SARAH stands.

ELGAH and AARON remain seated, eyes closed.

In a half circle around them, at the edges of the stage,
stand FIVE CREATURES.

They breathe throatily.

The CREATURES take a step towards SARAH.

Pause.

Another step.

Pause.

The CREATURES stop their throaty breathing.

Pause.

A bolt of lightning flashes, thunder cracks.

SARAH shrieks, falls to the floor.

The thunder and lightning increases.

The CREATURES step up to SARAH.

Drag her off-stage.

The thunder and lightning dies.

A huge growl resounds.

Silence.

ELGAH and AARON open their eyes.

A snuffling sound.

The two turn.

A CREATURE enters from the rear of the stage.

It is joined, one by one, by the other four.

Pause.

> CREATURE #1
> Help.
>
> CREATURE #2
> Help me.
>
> CREATURE #3
> Help.

The voices are plaintive, pitiful, pleading.

By degrees all FIVE CREATURES start calling the two phrases, over and over again with the voices of the sad, the lost, the hurt.

AARON and ELGAH stand

ELGAH takes a step towards the creatures.

Simultaneously with her step, the CREATURES stop calling.

Silence.

The CREATURES shuffle forwards.

AARON takes a step towards them.

The creatures halt.

AARON and ELGAH adopt a back-to-back position.

They close their eyes.

The CREATURES return to their original positions at the rear of the stage.

AARON and ELGAH sit, cross-legged, back-to-back.

The five CREATURES slowly back off the stage.

Silence.

SARAH enters.

Halts in the middle of the stage.

Pause.

She abruptly turns and runs towards one wing, is thrown back as if she had hit an elastic wall, falls onto the floor.

She sobs.

A CREATURE enters.

SARAH looks up, sees it, stands, runs away from it towards the other wing, is bounced back onto the stage, falls, renews her sobbing.

The CREATURE watches her.

SARAH stops sobbing.

Stands.

Walks over to the CREATURE.

Kneels at its feet.

The CREATURE turns, walks off.

SARAH stands, follows it off.

A howl.

JACOB enters.

AARON and ELGAH open their eyes.

Look towards JACOB.

Stand.

JACOB takes a step towards them.

They step back.

He takes another step towards them.

They take another step back.

JACOB halts, looks at them pleadingly.

Three creatures enter, halt.

JACOB becomes aware of their presence, looks at them over his shoulder, turns back to face AARON and ELGAH.

The CREATURES step towards JACOB.

He falls at the feet of AARON and ELGAH.

JACOB
Help me. Please.

CREATURES
Help me. Please. Please help me. Help. Help
me.

The CREATURES continue calling as they step
towards JACOB.
AARON steps between the CREATURES and JACOB.
The CREATURES stop calling, halt.
Pause.
AARON steps forwards.
The CREATURES step back.
AARON steps forwards.
The CREATURES step back.
AARON takes two steps forwards.
The CREATURES return to the rear of the stage.
Pause.
Thunder and lightning.
A growl.
The CREATURES back off-stage.
Enter JALAM, backwards.
He motions with his arm.
The thunder and lightning dies.
JALAM approaches JACOB, puts a hand on his
shoulder.
Turns, goes to his position, sits.
ELGAH and AARON embrace JACOB.
SARAH enters at rear of stage.
Halts.
ELGAH, JACOB and AARON turn towards SARAH
Examine her.
ELGAH takes a step towards SARAH,.
ELGAH extends her arms towards her.

SARAH hisses.

ELGAH steps back, re-joins the others.

SARAH motions with her arm.

Five CREATURES appear, stand in a line behind her at the rear of the stage.

Pause.

Abruptly, one of the CREATURES runs at the three.

AARON raises his hand.

The CREATURE hits an invisible wall, staggers, falls, is still.

Silence.

Two more CREATURES run at the three.

AARON, ELGAH and JACOB each raise a hand.

The two CREATURES hit an invisible wall, stagger, fall, lie still.

Silence.

The two remaining CREATURES slowly approach the invisible wall, with outstretched hands find its position, work their way around it, one to the left, the other to the right.

AARON remains facing SARAH.

ELGAH and JACOB each face one of the two creatures, circling with them.

The two CREATURES meet at the front of the stage.

They push against the invisible wall.

ELGAH and JACOB motion with their arms.

The two are thrown backwards, fall, are still.

Pause.

SARAH hisses.

The FIVE CREATURES stand, return to the rear of the stage.

The CREATURES exit.

Pause.

JALAM opens his eyes.

Stands.

JALAM looks at each of AARON, ELGAH and JACOB.

His gaze returns to AARON.

AARON nods.

ELGAH and JACOB embrace AARON separately.

JALAM approaches the edge of the stage slowly, as if wading against some kind of force.

He halts, holds out his hand.

ELGAH approaches JALAM, grasps his hand, holds out her own.

JACOB approaches, grasps ELGAH'S hand.

The three exit, slowly.

AARON and SARAH face each other.

SARAH hisses.

Lunges towards AARON.

AARON easily evades her.

SARAH lunges again—her movements are jagged, uncoordinated, as if whatever is in her body can't control it.

AARON evades her easily.

Pause.

SARAH circles AARON.

He follows her movements, continuing to face her.

SARAH abruptly runs at AARON.

AARON raises his hand.

SARAH stops, held in invisible bonds which she strains against but can't break.

A growl, off.

AARON lowers his arm.

SARAH is released.

SARAH staggers, runs towards one wing, bounces off it, runs to the other wing, bounces off that, runs around stage, explodes.

Her smoking body falls to the floor.

Pause.

Two CREATURES enter at rear – in contrast to the other times they have appeared, now they are hesitant.

The creatures approach SARAH'S body, cower beside it.

AARON motions.

The creatures drag the body off-stage.

As they exit a single human shriek is heard.

Silence.

Music.

Lights flashing, above.

JALAM, ELGAH and JACOB are seen above.

As they move out of sight, the flashing lights and music fade.

Pause.

A growl.

A clap of thunder, a flash of lightning.

They build slowly.

Voices, off.

> VOICES
> Help. Help me. Please, please help me.

Enter JOASH, ZEBAH, NAOMI.

They are frightened, uncertain.

The voices continue, getting louder, more hysterical.

The three approach AARON.

He sits.

Closes his eyes.

The three huddle near him.

A howl.

AARON motions with his arm.

All sound cuts.

Slow fade to black.

The Saviour

CHARACTERS

ESCAPEE 1
ESCAPEE 2
ESCAPEE 3
FREEMAN
SAVIOUR

SETTING

A stylised landscape containing a mound, a tree
with stick-like branches and no leaves. Remnants of
civilisation lie around – for example, a helmet, half a
wagon wheel, an oxen skull, a piece of tent dangling
from a pole. Soft yellow light shines from one
direction, suggesting dawn. The light that shines from
above is sharply defined and white.

Darkness.

A siren is turned on.

It howls.

A spotlight is switched on.

It roams the auditorium.

The sound of dogs barking approaches.

The sound of men tramping approaches.

The sound of tramping moves away. Dies.

The sound of dogs barking moves away. Dies.

The spotlight halts in the middle of the stage.

The siren dies.

Lights come up as the spotlight fades.

Silence.

Enter ESCAPEE 1 carrying a crucifixion crossbar across his shoulders, to which his wrists are tied.

He halts.

Looks to left.

Looks to right.

Sits.

Looks out at audience.

Sighs.

Looks down.

Pause.

Sound above, of a door opening – simultaneously light is cast onto the stage from above and a choir is heard singing.

ESCAPEE 1 stands.

Looks to left.

Looks to right.

Looks up.

Closes his eyes.

His lips move silently.

The shadow of a hand is cast onto the stage, drops a small box which falls to the stage.

The door slams shut, the light vanishes, the choir stops singing.

ESCAPEE 1 looks at the small box.

Walks to it.

Reaches down with one hand.

Takes out a cigarette.

Straightens.

Holding the cigarette in the fingers of one hand, leans towards it with his lips.

Can't reach it.

Hold.

Leans back.

Reflects.

Leans again towards the cigarette with his lips.

Strains, can't reach it.

Leans back.

Hold.

Sits.

Looks at the audience.

Looks down.

Sighs.

Pause.

Sound of dogs barking, off.

ESCAPEE 1 stands.

Runs to a corner of the stage and attempts futilely to hide.

The sound of the barking dogs approaches.

Diminishes.

Dies.

Enter ESCAPEE 2. He has a crossbar across his shoulders, to which his wrists are tied.

ESCAPEE 1 steps forwards.

The two ESCAPEES look at one another.

They simultaneously turn towards the audience.

Simultaneously sit, side by side.

Look at the audience.

Sigh.

Look down.

Pause.

ESCAPEE 2 looks up.

> ESCAPEE 2
> Nice view.

Silence.

ESCAPEE 2 looks at ESCAPEE 1.

ESCAPEE 1 looks at ESCAPEE 2.

ESCAPEE 1 holds out the cigarette.

ESCAPEE 2 shakes his head.

Pause.

> ESCAPEE 1
> God! What I'd give for a light!

> FREEMAN
> (Off) Brother, lament no longer.

Enter FREEMAN.

ESCAPEE 1 and ESCAPEE 2 stand.

FREEMAN pulls out a lighter, flicks it on, holds out a flame.

ESCAPEE 1 looks at it.

Looks at the cigarette between his fingers.

Moves the cigarette to just in front in the flame.

Moves it away.

Holds his face before the flame.

Leans away.

Looks at the cigarette between his fingers.

ESCAPEE 2:
You're not like us.

FREEMAN:
Brother, under the skin we're all the same.

ESCAPEE 1 drops the cigarette.

ESCAPEE 2:
But you're free.

FREEMAN:
Freedom is a state of mind.

ESCAPEE 2:
I had a mind once.

ESCAPEE 1 kneels, picks up the cigarette with his lips.

FREEMAN
Be careful, brother. The sin of vanity waits to
strangle us all.

ESCAPEE 2
I asked for strangulation. Anything but hanging
up there in the boiling sun, waiting for the life to
slowly drain out of you.

FREEMAN
Time is one of the great mysteries.

ESCAPEE 1 stands, cigarette between his lips.

ESCAPEE 2
Merciful death, strangulation. They said I wasn't
worthy of it. I'm a commoner. Too common for the
mercy of strangulation.

ESCAPEE 1 approaches the lighter flame.

FREEMAN

Brother, the soul is the real bestower of aristocracy.
And the aristocracy of the soul means that
underneath we're all – good lord, look at that!

Just as ESCAPEE 1 is about to light the cigarette FREEMAN
snaps the lighter shut, steps forwards, looks out at the
audience.

FREEMAN

What a view!

FREEMAN's attention is attracted by movement in the
auditorium.
ESCAPEE 1 and ESCAPEE 2 attempt to hide.
FREEMAN continues looking out into the auditorium.
Enter ESCAPEE 3, through the audience. He has a
crucifixion crossbar across his shoulders, to which his
wrists are tied.
ESCAPEE 3 comes on stage.
ESCAPEE 1 and ESCAPEE 2 approach.
All stare at ESCAPEE 3.
ESCAPEE 3 stares back at them.
Pause.
The three ESCAPEES simultaneously turn.
Stand in a line facing the audience.
Sit.
Look at the audience.
Look down.
Sigh.
Silence.

ESCAPEE 1

God's a bastard.

FREEMAN

Impossible. You've escaped death. You're not
suffering. Or in pain. And you have a wonderful view.

ESCAPEE 1

I can prove it.

The others simultaneously turn towards ESCAPEE 1.
ESCAPEE 1 looks above, closes his eyes. His lips move in
silent prayer.
The door above opens, light is cast onto the stage, the
choir sings.
The shadow of a hand is cast onto the stage, holding a
small box.
The box drops onto the stage.
The door slams, the light is cut, the choir stops.
FREEMAN picks up the box.
Takes out a cigarette lighter.

FREEMAN

You've lost, brother.

ESCAPEE 1 indicates the cigarette between his lips.
ESCAPEE 3 takes the lighter from FREEMAN,
approaches ESCAPEE 1, repeatedly attempts to ignite the
lighter.
Nothing happens.

ESCAPEE 3

No fluid.

ESCAPEE 2

The bastard.

ESCAPEE 1

I rest my case.

> FREEMAN
> Brothers, God is telling us something.

The three look at FREEMAN.
Look at each other.
Turn towards the audience.

> FREEMAN
> He wants us to pray to him.

> ESCAPEE 3
> What for?

> FREEMAN
> A saviour to ignite our lives.

All turn and look at FREEMAN.
FREEMAN turns and looks at ESCAPEE 1.
All turn and look at ESCAPEE 1.
Pause.
ESCAPEE 1 looks above, closes his eyes.
His lips move in a silent prayer.
The door above opens, light pours down onto the stage, the choir sings.
The light illuminates an action: from the wings a cross wheels onto the stage, on which hangs a crucified SAVIOUR.
The cross comes to a halt.
Hold.
The door slams, the light cuts, the choir stops.
The four stare at the SAVIOUR.
Pause.
They turn, facing the audience in a line.
Sit.
Look out at audience.
Look down.

Sigh.
ESCAPEE 3 starts to laugh.
Presently he stops.
ESCAPEE 2 sobs.
Presently he stops.
Silence.
The SAVIOUR moans.
FREEMAN stands.
Approaches the SAVIOUR.
Listens.

>SAVIOUR
>Lur – Lurve – one – uh –

>ESCAPEE 3
>What's he saying?

>FREEMAN
>Lur – lurve.

>SAVIOUR
>Lur – Lurve – uh – ther –

>FREEMAN
>Love.

>SAVIOUR
>One – uh – one – u – ther –

>FREEMAN
>Love one another.

>ESCAPEE 2
>Think it will work?

FREEMAN turns, looks at the three.
The three look at each other.

Pause.

FREEMAN returns.

Sits.

All four look out at audience.

Sigh.

Look down.

Silence.

> SAVIOUR
> Dad?

Pause.

> SAVIOUR
> Dad!

The door above opens, light shines down, the choir sings.

> SAVIOUR
> I warned you this would happen.

Hold.

> SAVIOUR
> It's over!

The door above closes, the choir stops, the light cuts.

Silence.

The SAVIOUR climbs down off the cross, the crossbar strapped across his shoulders.

He steps off the stage, walks through the auditorium.

Exits.

Silence.

ESCAPEE 1 stands.

Approaches the cross.

Looks up at it.

Drops the cigarette.

Climbs up onto the cross.

The others simultaneously stand, turn, watch him.

ESCAPEE 1 hangs crucified.

Pause.

The siren starts.

A spotlight switches on.

The sound of dogs barking.

This sound approaches.

The sound of marching men.

This sound approaches.

The spotlight roves around the auditorium.

The three run around the stage.

They end together in the centre of the stage.

The spotlight finds them, holds.

Abruptly, all sound cuts.

> VOICE (Off, through loud-hailer)
> Do not move. Separate from each another. Keep your hands visible at all times.

ESCAPEE 2, ESCAPEE 3 and FREEMAN stand.

Form a line facing the audience.

> VOICE (Off, through loud-hailer)
> One. Two. Three. All escapees found and accounted for.

> FREEMAN
> You're making a mistake. I'm not one of them. I'm a freema –

> VOICE (Off, through loud-hailer)
> Silence! Escapees. To the right, turn! Quick march!

The three turn, march off the stage, the spotlight moving with them.

ESCAPEE 1 remains on the cross.

The spotlight is switched off.

Silence.

Noises off, of nails being driven into wood, accompanied by three sets of screams.

The blows stop.

The screams die.

Pause.

Sobs, off.

Continue.

Fade.

Silence.

ESCAPEE 1 looks above.

Hold.

Looks at audience.

Hold.

Slow fade to black.

Interrogations  [2022]

A Creative History

Why are we concerned with art? To cross our frontiers,
exceed our limitations, fill our emptiness – fulfil ourselves.
This is not a condition but a process, in which what is
dark in us slowly becomes transparent. In this struggle
with one's own truth, the theatre has always seemed to me
a place of provocation. – Jerzy Grotowski

This collection presents a selection from my early mostly unpublished writing. The work reflects my interest in exploring border
zones where literature, history, religion, psychology and spirituality
intersect. Culturally and intellectually, we are still working through
the implications of the shift initiated by seventeenth century En-
lightenment thinkers, from a mythological, supernatural world view
to a rational, naturalist outlook. My interest is in how those who
view humanity as possessing a spiritual dimension have responded
to this shift. In particular, how they have critiqued collective beliefs,
deconstructed religious narratives, generated meaning on the basis of personal numinous experience, and striven for self-transcen-
dence. William Blake shows how artists may integrate spirituality
into their work by giving the imagination spiritual as well as artistic
value. Many twentieth century thinkers and writers – Rainer Maria
Rilke, Samuel Beckett, Carl Jung, D.T. Suzuki, Evelyn Underwood,
Elaine Pagels, Gary Snyder, Jacques Derrida, Karen Armstrong, to
name an arbitrarily chosen handful – have explored aspects of this
extensive psychospiritual territory.

In the early 1980s I came across Jerzy Grotowski's *Towards a
Poor Theatre*, in which he outlined his theory and practice for
creating performance art. Much of what he wrote resonated with
me. To repeat the question he asked, and his answer: 'Why are we
concerned with art? To cross our frontiers, exceed our limitations,
fill our emptiness – fulfil ourselves. This is not a condition but a
process in which what is dark in us slowly becomes transparent.'

Grotowski's answer is aspirational, not programmatic. It is sufficiently generalised that it leaves space for personal application. What frontiers? That depends on where we are situated physically, culturally, psychologically, artistically. Which limitations? They depend on our social context, the cultural prohibitions we face, our family upbringing, and our own psychological traits. What emptiness? A feeling of emptiness is the manifestation of an inner lack. We each lack different things in different ways. What fulfilment? We seek fulfilment depending on what we feel we lack, what intrigues us, what we feel driven to engage with, and what we decide we need to acquire or develop in order to fill our emptiness.

We are complex social, psychological and spiritual beings. We are each 'put together' differently. We respond personally – very personally – to the experience of being in the world, and as a result are attracted to particular modes of connection, expression and creation ... or withdrawal, introversion, destruction. These are not fixed modalities. We swing between them depending on what social situations we find ourselves in, and according to our innate predispositions, particularly the character traits that push us to respond to life circumstances in the ways we do.

Innate predispositions do not just differentiate one artist from another, but draw each of us individually to the particular situations, experiences and ideas that resonate most intensely within us as we engage with the world and strive towards fulfilment. Complicating the situation is that complete fulfilment is a state we rarely, if ever, attain. Yet humanity's striving to achieve this (im)possible goal has created a marvellously rich tapestry of artistic accomplishments woven across the millennia. Like many others, I have used artistic creation to aesthetically embody my attempts to vault limitations, breach new frontiers, replenish my emptiness, and fulfil at least a portion of my potential as a human being.

Thus the work presented here has a dual focus. First, it embodies my reflections on a number of tensions that have resulted from the post-Enlightenment project of establishing a rational, naturalistic view of reality. (I have explored how this has impacted on our ideas about God in *The God Revolution* and morality in *Striving To Be Human*.) Second, it is the artistic expression of my interrogation of cultural, psychological and spiritual factors that have shaped me personally, as a human being born in an English-speaking Western nation in the second half of the twentieth century.

A Brief History of the World

The four plays that constitute *A Brief History of the World* have their roots in my thinking about Christianity's impact on the Western psyche. The doctrines foundational to Christianity – God as rewarding and punishing Father; Adam and Eve's sin of eating an apple in the Garden of Eden, which led to God exiling all humanity; and the arrival and departure of God's son, in whom we are required to believe before God will forgive our sins – took shape over the course of several centuries.

To offer an example: In the fourth century Augustine formulated the doctrine of original sin. This doctrine defines human beings as being born in and of sin. Generations of Christians have been taught from childhood that spiritually they are corrupt, and if they fail to live in accord with their church's strictures they will be punished forever. This has led to each generation growing up with deep-seated feelings of inadequacy and guilt.

That negative psychospiritual stance was compounded when the early Church adopted the strategy of crushing all competing ideas. (Of course, crushing the competition is not unique to Christianity.) The early Church condemned as heretics those who diverged from orthodox doctrine and burned their books. In 1557 the Papal Office went so far as to create the *Index Librorum Prohibitorum* (*List of Prohibited Books*), which sought to protect believers from modern thinking by banning them from reading the writings of leading scientists and philosophers, including Galileo, Bacon, Descartes, Hume, Kant, Voltaire, Spinoza and Darwin. The *Index* survived until 1966.

The strategy of controlling people via prohibition may be basic to Christianity, but it is not unique to it. Following the rise of city-states during the Bronze Age, entire populations faced prohibition on the grounds of cultural, religious, political, racial and gender difference, which led to slavery, torture and massacre. Prohibition was adopted by European nations when they colonised the rest of the world, using zealous believers and Parliamentary decree to suppress indigenous traditions and practices. Christian attitudes were then embedded in those colonised countries' cultural, legal, economic, educational and political institutions, ensuring they remain active even in today's secular states. The recent phenomena of cancel culture is a variety of prohibition, arguably having its antecedent in Christianity, which cancelled the souls of the disapproved. *A Brief History of the World* interrogates the implications.

This returns me to the end of the quotation from Grotowski: 'In this struggle with one's own truth the theatre has always seemed to me a place of provocation.' If artists are to interrogate the 'truths' gifted to them by their culture, and establish a 'truth' of their own, then their art, by definition, will be confrontational. It will question and doubt. Questioning and doubting are inevitably viewed as provocative by those committed to what is being questioned. Yet the purpose is not to capriciously insult or petulantly undermine. Rather, it is to ask vital questions: Where are we? How did we get here? What are we to do here? And to what extent is guilt, or fear, or ignorance, holding us back from challenging and changing the psychospiritual status quo? *The Catalogue of An Ordinary Life* explores these questions in dramatic form.

The Catalogue of an Ordinary Life

The theatrical models on which I drew when conceiving this play are the late medieval English Wakefield Pageants in the Towneley Cycle, two Samuel Beckett one-act plays, and Peter Handke's *The Ride Across Lake Constance*.

Medieval morality plays created symbolic characters to dramatise Christian doctrine. The most famous example is *Everyman*. God sends Death to remind Everyman of his inevitable end and the danger of being eternally condemned: 'In hell for to dwell, world without end.' (Late medieval Christianity preferred to picture the torments of hell over the pleasures of heaven, punishment over reward.) After Death's visit Everyman asks Fellowship, Kindred, Good, Confession, Beauty, Strength and Discretion to accompany him. Each refuses. Even his Wits depart. Finally, he is left with only his Good Deeds, and Knowledge as observer.

This is all conventional religious allegory. In contrast, the Wakefield Pageants, while theologically orthodox, offer a more complex, even subversive, theatrical experience. Low comedy rubs shoulders with material drawn from the liturgy, sophisticated poetry is juxtaposed to colloquial dialogue, and action often veers into farce. One striking moment occurs when two shepherds go to Bethlehem to pay tribute to the new-born Jesus, the Lamb of God, and discover an actual sheep in the manger.

Despite this irreverence, the Wakefield Pageants reinforce the late medieval view that humanity's state is static: an individual's social position is for life, all spiritual knowledge has been given, and, like God, it is complete and perfect, with nothing needing to be added. Humanity has just two fundamental choices, believe or not, and two spiritual outcomes, be saved or be condemned.

Medieval morality plays are symbolic, being designed to dramatise a world view. By the early twentieth century the old medieval feudal social, religious and intellectual certainties had broken down. A void ensued, which was filled by the art, literature, music and theatre of the avant-garde. Expressionist theatre replaced the medieval Everyman with the New Man, a symbolic representative of what humanity could/should achieve. Presenting characters who are symbolic rather than naturalistic, types rather than individuals, was also adopted by other avant-garde theatres, including epic theatre, the theatre of the absurd, and the theatre of Samuel Beckett.

Eschewing social and political agendas, Beckett created a meta-physical theatre (that denied metaphysics) as he strove to depict humanity at its most fundamental. *Waiting for Godot* is an obvious example. But I was drawn to two of Beckett's one-act plays, *Act Without Words* I and II. In these plays gesture entirely replaces dialogue.

In *Act Without Words* I the single performer is guided by a whistle. Various objects appear on stage: a palm tree, a pair of nail scissors, boxes, a carafe labelled WATER, but when the performer attempts to use the objects they are withdrawn. Eventually, despite repeated whistles, the performer refuses to respond, leaving the audience with a number of questions. Is the refusal to engage with an inscrutable, possibly malevolent, off-stage will, an acknowledge-ment of defeat, an act of submission, a posture of defiance, or out-right rebellion?

Act Without Words II depicts the implied off-stage malevolence more explicitly. Two sacks sit on the stage. A goad on wheels reach-es from a wing and pokes first one sack, then the other. From each sack emerges a performer who carries out a series of actions. The first swallows pills, prays, and eats a carrot, which is spat out in disgust. This performer then moves the sack across the stage, away from the goad, and climbs back in. The second performer regularly consults a watch, and uses a map and compass to decide where to move the second sack. The performer finally moves it beside that of the first, and climbs into it. The goad appears once again, poking the first performer, who emerges and begins to repeat the previous routine, at which point the play ends.

What fascinated me about these two plays is their reliance on gesture over dialogue, characters' reduction to basic motivation, the minimalism of the props that suggests significance without disclos-ing any, and their brevity, exploring just a single theatrical idea.

Peter Handke's *The Ride across Lake Constance* offers a more complex combination of specificity and abstraction. The play's set-ting is a bourgeois room, and the characters are famous film actors and directors. Yet they are not presented naturalistically. Instead, they express a series of disjointed emotional attitudes, tell stories, make jokes, and indulge in slapstick, all of which refuses to develop into a narrative or to make a coherent thematic statement.

When conceiving *The Catalogue of an Ordinary Life*, I drew on the meta-theatrical approach of the medieval mystery plays and Beckett – acknowledging that for medieval authors an (intermittently) benevolent God exists beyond the confines of the world, while for Beckett some kind of impersonal meta-drive exists beyond the confines of the stage, which refuses to reveal itself and is at best indifferent, at worst malevolent.

To this sense of an ambiguous meta-reality, I added a setting that reflected the specificity of Handke's play, while avoiding making the onstage characters naturalistic. Rather, they represent attitudes, their dramatic interactions are fundamentally gestural, and dialogue consists of cliché. Thematically, the play explores conformity, repression and our participation in that repression.

Innerworld of the Underworld

The title of this play derives from Handke, Beckett's gestural theatre is taken even further than in the preceding play, the drama explores the madness that heaves in the basement of the human psyche, and the theatrical treatment draws on Antonin Artaud's ideas. In *The Theatre and Its Double*, Artaud writes: 'Our sensibility has reached a point where we surely need theatre that wakes up hearts and nerves.' To achieve that goal Artaud sought to create a visceral form of theatre that is physically, emotionally and spiritually transporting. He called it the theatre of cruelty. This is not cruelty in the sense of sadistically provoking pain:

> The word cruelty must be used in its broadest sense, not
> in the physical, predatory sense usually ascribed to it. ... I
> use the word cruelty in the sense of hungering after life,
> cosmic strictness, relentless necessity, in the gnostic sense

of a living vortex engulfing darkness, in the sense of the inescapably necessary pain without which life could not continue.

Artaud developed his concept of theatre after witnessing the combination of dance, music and gesture practised in Balinese folk theatre. He was also inspired by Alfred Jarry, who was revered as a forerunner by the Dadaists and Surrealists. Jarry's theatrical masterpiece is *Ubu Roi* (*King Ubu*), which I first saw as a Polish animated film. Inspired by puppetry, the play was originally written with a school friend when Jarry was fifteen. One scene from the *Ubu* plays has stayed with me. Ubu carries a suitcase, inside which is his conscience. Periodically, he opens the suitcase to consult his conscience. Usually, it tells him what he doesn't want to hear and he ignores it. Eventually, disgusted with its advice, he flushes his conscience down the toilet. *Ubu Roi* was denounced by critics on its première in 1896 – a première attended by W.B. Yeats, who defended its spirited attack on the bourgeois, but lamented it signalled an artistic shift from the subtle symbolist spirituality he championed to the crude, grotesque comedy of what he called 'the Savage God'. Yet after the grotesqueries of World War One, it was the Savage God who proved the most relevant to those who wished to interrogate the time. Jarry, by then seven years dead, was revealed to be prescient beyond even his own wildest prognostications.

It could be said that Yeats' Savage God was turned inside out and vitally re-energised by Artaud. Where Jarry used humour and the grotesque to expose and confront bourgeois values, Artaud sought to give the audience an experience that transported them through normative values to discover the 'living vortex' that lay on their far side. Artaud's use of the word gnostic in relation to this vortex is significant. Gnostic may be understood in two senses. The English word gnostic is derived from the Greek *gnosis*, knowledge. During Christianity's foundational period, from the first to sixth centuries, a spiritual movement adopted the term gnosis to refer to experientially acquired spiritual knowledge. These spiritual seekers consequently became known as Gnostics; scholars later denoted their spiritual outlook Gnosticism. Hence, upper-case Gnostic refers to the historical spiritual movement that overlapped with early Christianity, while lower-case gnostic refers to deep insights and knowledge obtained via direct experience. When Artaud writes that he uses 'the word cruelty ... in the gnostic sense of a living vortex engulfing darkness', he is adopting this second, non-historic sense.

As an experience, gnosis can be illuminative and experienced via light, or extracted from pain-filled darkness. Artaud's theatre of cruelty explores this second course. His purpose is to 'wake up hearts and nerves'. Confrontation with the dark domains of our individual and collective psyches is central to Artaud's theatrical project. Similarly, *Innerworld of the Underworld* confronts darkness and madness, and seeks to use the tools of symbolic theatre – gesture, voice, sound, tableau – to situate the audience inside 'the living vortex of darkness' and to explore how it may be acknowledged, confronted and pacified.

The play's epigraph is taken from *The Gospel According to Thomas*, a possibly first century Gnostic text found in Nag Hammadi, Egypt, in 1945. The epigraph states: 'Blessed is the lion the man eats and the lion will become a man; and cursed is the man the lion eats and the lion will become a man.' My reading of this is that the lion symbolises the human psyche's bestial, territorial, violent nature. Human beings who control this part of their psyche integrate it into their being, and so 'the lion will become a man.' Conversely, those who do not establish control find their psyche is overwhelmed (cursed), their higher human capacities are diminished, and bestial, territorial and violent traits dominate their behaviour to such a degree that 'the lion will become a man'.

Accordingly, *Innerworld of the Underworld* may be read as a symbolic dramatisation of the struggle between our lower and higher impulses, a struggle that is repeated by each generation. Artaud's theatre of cruelty was appropriate for presenting this conflict, given he sought 'to express objectively secret truths, to bring out in active gestures those elements of truth hidden under forms in their encounters with becoming'.

When considering how to dramatise this struggle through darkness towards a higher level of becoming, my mind turned to the ancient Hebrew historical and prophetic books. The God in these books is dark, demanding and destructive: encouraging Abraham to prove his faith by killing his own son; razing the cities of Sodom and Gomorrah; and decreeing death for children who disobeyed their parents, those who worked on the Sabbath, and whoever engaged in premarital sex. Today we view these last punishments as the inventions of human beings who justify control of others by claiming they are demanded by God. These are oppressive and tyrannical impulses to which no single individual, nation or era may lay an ascendant claim. Accordingly, while I have given Jewish names to the characters in this play, the play is intended to offer a generalised dramatisation of one aspect of the human psyche, and not to comment on any particular time, history or people.

Innerworld of the Underworld is an experiment. I have not seen it in performance, so have not been able to gauge its success as theatre. However, if the performers find an effective dance-like gestural modality in their actions, and if the aural and lighting effects surround the audience, situating them in the middle of the drama, I anticipate the experience will be of the 'living vortex of devouring darkness' to which Artaud refers.

Waymarks

The collection now shifts to my earliest surviving writing. In the early 1970s I was dissatisfied with life. I was in my teens, living in Auckland's suburbs, but what I craved was to be taken far beyond my everyday, mundane, constricted reality. Books provided transportation. In 1973 a school friend introduced me to three nineteenth century French poets, Rimbaud, Baudelaire and Lautremont. I fell under their heady spell. I was especially intrigued by their excesses: Rimbaud's decision to become a visionary by systematically deranging his senses; Baudelaire's call to always be drunk, with poetry, with wine, even with virtue (which he elegantly, contrarily, and with a decadent élan, subverted); and Lautremont's imaginative extravagance, including a fantastical description of having sex with a shark in the ocean. They led to the work of the Surrealists, who promoted the virtues of visionary experience that transcended, or at least ran parallel to, everyday life.

I was particularly struck by the work of San Francisco poet, Philip Lamantia. Lamantia performed in one of Maya Deren's experimental films (scored by John Cage), and took part in the reading during which Allen Ginsberg première *Howl*. Following the lead of Baudelaire and Rimbaud, to whom he addressed early poems, Lamantia used narcotics to enter ecstatic states and stimulate visionary experiences. This led him in 1959 to publish *Narcotica*, which celebrated the virtues of taking drugs and inveighed against repressive anti-drug laws. Artaud contributed two pieces. In later years, Lamantia explored various esoteric and mystical fields, including Hermeticism, Gnosticism and the sacred geometry Schwaller de Lubicz discovered in ancient Egyptian buildings. I didn't know this when I first read Lamantia's poems, but several years later I was also drawn to these fields, and so followed Lamantia's footsteps, though adopting a very different trajectory.

My interest in esoteric spirituality developed in 1975, when I joined a gnostic group led by a New Zealander, Abdullah Dougan. (The group is satirised by C.K. Stead in his novel, *The Death of the Body*.) Abdullah taught the developmental practices of G.I. Gurdjieff and the Sufis. Gnostic group meetings (gnostic in the general sense) provided a practical means for exploring the depths that I sensed existed around and within me, but didn't know how to access. The meetings included readings from classic texts of Sufism, Buddhism, Taoism, Zoroastrianism, Gnosticism and Advaita Vedanta. These readings offered an appreciation of how our forebears explored and described the transcendent aspects of human experience. They stimulated an interest that manifested years later in my working on several world mystical texts.

The exhilaration I felt at this time is reflected in the poems collected in *Waymarks*. They present concepts drawn from Gurdjieff and Sufism, set in symbolic landscapes and cityscapes. The idea of symbolic settings was inspired by Blake's paintings, which he declared were not copied from nature but were seen with the eye of the imagination.

The greatest curiosity here – possibly to the reader, and certainly to me at the time – are the prose poems. In Idries Shah's seminal study *The Sufis* I came across the following passage, which Shah translated from a poem written by the twelfth century Sufi Lal Shahbaz Qalander, popularly known as Mast Qalander ('intoxicated dervish'):

> The Creator from the spreading of fervour and the essence of religious feeling thus ordered the 'juice of the grape' for the breakfasting of the Lovers (Sufis), and in the sacramental bread of the half understanders he left a symbol. .... And the breakfasting was of the breakfast of truths on the way of uncrackedness. Finally, after the spreading (vine) and grape came, and after its juice made wine, and supping (after abstinence), the Complete Man was made, fashioned strangely by the blunt scimitar. But this bread is not from what they say, neither from beneath the tree. Truly the Truth of Creation is discovered and ecstasy may be solely known in this hiddenness of the bread of the hungry and thirsty. His drink is after his food. The Creator displays as the opener.

This rapturous outpouring struck me for several reasons. Like Surrealist poetry, it evokes a sense of hallucinatory intoxication. This doesn't appeal to everyone: Shah observes that in the twelfth century the above passage was considered 'the ravings of a madman'. However, it possesses an internal logic that makes its intoxication different from the intoxications of the Surrealists.

Influenced by Freud's theory of the unconscious, Andre Breton, Surrealism's founder and primary theorist, encouraged writers and artists to practise psychic automatism, by-passing rational thinking to draw on unconscious elements within the mind, using them to create. Breton also embraced dreams and madness – the latter understandably, given that civilised 'sanity' had generated the social and political conditions that led to World War One. Breton was a medical orderly, so witnessed first-hand the horrors of war. After peace was declared, Breton, like the rest of the European avant-garde, strove to crawl out of the cultural, psychological and intellectual craters war had blasted, eager to find new ways to think and feel. Thus the Surrealists welcomed madness: no longer pretending to be sane was a sane response to the 'menacing machine' (Lamantia's phrase) that is the modern world. Delirium and ecstasy offered psychic modalities conducive to creating a new world.

In the goal of creating a new world, Sufis have an advantage over Surrealists, because they have a practical process for transforming the psyche, dismantling its self-limiting and self-destructive tendencies, and inwardly generating a transformed human being. To describe this psychospiritual process of transformation, the Sufis developed a complex symbolic language that draws on religion, morality, philosophy, psychology and mysticism.

Clearly, 'the juice of the grape' is a symbolic expression. Wine is used by Sufis to symbolise spiritualised energy imbued with love and gnosis. Western wine symbolism probably dates to the cult of Dionysus, the Greek god of intoxication, self-abandonment and ecstasy. Dionysus was central to the Eleusinian Mysteries, which culminated in a visionary experience of the divine, aided by fasting and the likely ingestion of a psychedelic substance. The rituals concluded with a feast. This sacred meal, which itself derived from ancient harvest celebrations, was practised by all the ancient Mediterranean mystery cults, and was subsequently adopted by the

Abrahamic religions of Judaism, Christianity and Islam. The Sufis used the wine and bread imagery of sacred meals to symbolically reference the process of self-development. Thus in the excerpt from Mast Qalander's poem, the Complete Man – also known as the Perfect Man and the Man of Light ('Man' in a collective and not a gendered sense) – refers to the spiritually developed individual, and the blunt scimitar to the teaching that facilitates incremental inner transformation. The lovers are those committed to the process of inner transformation, while their breakfasting occurs when they share bread and wine, the food of gnostic experience.

It is worth comparing this Sufi approach to that of the Surrealists. This is the opening of Lamantia's poem, *I Am Coming*:

> I am following her to the wavering moon
> to a bridge by the long waterfront
> to valleys of beautiful arson
> to flowers dead in a mirror of love
> to men eating wild minutes from a clock
> to hands playing in celestial pockets
> and to that dark room beside a castle
> of youthful voices singing to the moon.

Mast Qalander and Lamantia each create a hallucinatory effect, but do so differently. In Lamantia's poem, each line presents an image, creating a surreal landscape through the accumulation of details. The move from one line to the next is achieved associatively, while the move is driven emotionally by the narrator's longing for a mysterious unnamed *her*. The poem's climax is an imagined arrival:

> But I am coming to the moon
> and she will be there in a musical night
> in a night of burning laughter
> burning like a road of my brain
> pouring its arm into the lunar lake.

The narrator longs for arrival, but the poem's lunar associations not only assert how physically distant she is, but suggest union is possible only in the mind.

In contrast, the Sufi passage achieves its hallucinatory effect through strangeness. Lamantia's landscape is strange too, but is constituted of elements we recognise in surreal juxtaposition: valleys of beautiful arson, flowers dead in a mirror, men eating wild minutes. The Sufi passage is strange because on first reading we don't recognise what it is referencing. The opening sentence suggests meaning will be delivered logically: the Creator prepares breakfast for lovers and bread for those starting out. Yet the text that follows does not present information in a logical, step-by-step fashion. Instead, an early phrase simply seems unhinged: 'the breakfast of truths on the way of uncrackedness'. The structure then becomes circular, building meaning by shifting around the central concepts of breakfast, bread and wine. The circular structure is made clear through the reference to the Creator in the first and last sentences.

To understand Lamantia, readers need to bring their imagination; to understand Mast Qalander they need to bring prior knowledge. This is because he uses initiatory language, which is designed to be opaque to those unfamiliar with Sufi terminology – opaqueness being necessary at a time when those promoting orthodoxy hunted out what they judged blasphemy. The virtue of symbolic language is that it is opaque to the uninitiated, while those in the process of being initiated into Sufic developmental practices find the language opens up as they themselves open up.

The combination of strangeness, and the fact I was myself beginning my own self-initiatory developmental process, was so attractive that I began a series of prose poems inspired by Mast Qalander's writing. Over a period of seven days I wrote ten. Artistically, my goal was to create prose poems that explored the mystical language I was being introduced to. I also sought a balance of Lamantia and Qalander, adopting the former's repetition and association, while circling around the subject like the latter.

The Passionate Pilgrim

Six weeks after experimenting with the prose poems, I started writing sonnets. The prose poems provided a lead in because while they free the poet from formal constraints, without consciously willing it I found myself incorporating rhythm and rhyme into them. When writing poetry previously, I had used the line to organise units of meaning. But in prose poems, the sentences don't have line lengths. Wanting to give each sentence formal pressure, I found myself instinctively utilising rhythm and rhyme. That I should go on to attempt writing in a traditional poetic form was therefore a natural outgrowth of experimenting with prose poems.

At this time I was enamoured of Shakespeare's sonnets. The challenge of writing a sonnet is that it requires formal discipline, intellectual precision and exact articulation. The Shakespearean sonnet, containing three quatrains concluded by a couplet, is formally a vehicle whereby a statement is made, then elaborated or contradicted. It ends with a conclusion that either arrives at a different place emotionally and/or intellectually from where the poem began, or reinforces that start. I felt my previous poetry had been too emotional, too vague. I needed to sharpen my poetic processes, both by clarifying my thinking and by making the language more precise. As an aid to developing both the sonnet was ideal.

To my surprise, I found I had no difficulty coping with the form. Over a period of eight months I wrote fifty-six sonnets. Each was written in one sitting and given minimal reworking. As a result of such rapid composition, their success varies. Those I consider the best are included here. As an experiment they produced the sought effect. By imitating the patterns of Shakespeare's sonnets I quickly learned how to adjust my thinking to the pattern – this is an interesting creative situation in which form regulates thought. I also made useful discoveries about rhythm and language: Iambic pentameter naturally provides a rhythm that frees rather than constricts English poetic language. As a result of pushing the form to see how far it could stretch, I tried different structures, extending the opening statement across two quatrains, and even attempting a one sentence sonnet. In some sonnets I tried ignoring the metrical demands, concentrating on the voice over the meter. Poetically, writing iambic pentameter showed me its rhythmic and tonal possibilities. I returned to it several years later when choosing languages for *The Gnosis of Simon Magus* and the *Bhagavad Gita*.

Over the years I have shifted between the two genres of metaphysical poems and mystic love poems. Metaphysical poems focus on ideas, while mystical love poems explore experience. In the sonnets, I adopted Shakespeare's strategy of addressing a distant beloved. But where Shakespeare addresses his sonnets to human beings, I address a beloved who is variously, and sometimes simultaneously, my own spiritual self, God as abstract source, and the state of gnosis. Hence the sonnets do three things: they are intended to be love poems to the source, they reflect my exploration of world metaphysical concepts, and they are expressions of my personal spiritual quest.

Records of a Non-Plussed Being

Reviewing the sonnets, I was satisfied with fewer than half of them. I considered they had two faults: most relied too heavily on literary conventions and language, and many tended towards abstraction. I decided my next poems would counter this by using only concrete images and simple and direct language.

In considering this aim I was reminded of Ezra Pound's *Imagist Manifesto*, which I had studied at university. The Imagists' practice resonated because they were attempting to bring English poetry out of the Georgian era, replacing elaboration with simplicity, ornamentation with direct statement. They also rebelled against the constrictions of rhythm and rhyme, which they considered had made English poetry too predictable and enervated.

However, I didn't want to follow one aspect of the Imagists' practice: their advocacy of free verse. I had abandoned that approach in writing the sonnets, and wasn't inclined to return to it. What I needed was a form which didn't rhyme, but still had tight formal structure. One of the poetic traditions Pound referred to in his Imagist manifesto was Japanese haiku. I then discovered renga, linked haiku. This literary form ostensibly developed when poets got together, and one poet devised a haiku, to which the next responded. Renga is not linked intellectually, as with a sonnet. Rather, like Surrealist practice, the link is allusive, with the next haiku taking off from an image, an emotion, a play on words or a fleeting perception suggested by the previous haiku. So I had both a form and a formal method of construction.

I also realised that linked haiku has narrative possibilities. Around this time, as part of a Spanish course, I had been reading the poetry of Frederico Garcia Lorca. Drawing from Spanish folk songs, his work has an imagistic directness similar to Japanese poetry. Lorca's other talent was constructing narratives out of spare lyrical poetry, and achieving emotional power through reticence rather than over-statement. Lorca became another influence.

The final decision I made before beginning this sequence was that I wanted to move away from wallowing in personal emotions and thoughts. Almost all my poetry to that date had been about myself. I decided it was time to change tack and write about other people and their situations. Because I hadn't previously dealt poetically with the contemporary world, I decided the poems would be contemporary and metropolitan in setting. As well as exploring the possibilities for developing poetic narratives, for the first time my writing also included a satiric edge. This is a mode I subsequently returned to in other forms.

During my research into Japanese poetry, I came across Bashō and Issa, two of Japan's greatest poets. Both were associated with Zen Buddhism. Their haiku have been extensively anthologised, but they also pioneered haibun, prose embedded with haiku. Two of the greatest examples of the genre are Bashō's *Narrow Road to the*

Deep North and Issa's *A Year in the Life*. Bashō's work is structured as a journey through Japan, Issa's as a journal he kept from New Year to New Year. I was intrigued by the concept of combining poetry and prose, so decided to write a work of haibun to accompany the poems. Following Bashō's example, I structured it as a journey from the bottom of the South Island to the top of the North Island. Experiences I had while travelling during university holidays fed into this piece.

In one respect this sequence is a failure. Originally, its title was *Visons of the Children of Pain*. My idea was it would be the first in a series of seven works that paired a sequence of poems with a prose narrative. Thematically, the seven works would reflect the process of psychospiritual development. *Visions of the Children of Pain*, the first, focuses on the limitations of modern life, which leads to alienation and feelings of emptiness and futility. This is why the *Vision* poems are collectively depressed: psychologically, they depict human existence as a frustrating dead-end. I envisaged the second sequence, tentatively titled *Portraits of Confusion*, would explore our realising this and developing an inner need to emerge from it.

Where the *Visions* poems reflect an imagist approach, the *Portraits* sequence adopted a T.S. Eliot-influenced aesthetic. However, the resulting poems were too stylistically derivative, my ideas were too vague, and the work didn't coalesce. Accordingly, I abandoned both *Portraits of Confusion* and the seven work project.

This collection's opening prose piece, *On Green Dolphin Street*, is excerpted from the abandoned *Portraits* prose work. But I didn't abandon the project's underlying developmental idea, returning to it when conceiving *Exile and Return*.

Mira's Tied Bells to Her Ankles

In 1979 I visited an ashram in Rajasthan for six weeks. The ashram's founder, Shri Muniji Maharaj, proposed I work on translations of two Upanishads and poems he selected from the collections of two of India's greatest mystical poets, Mirabai and Kabir. The original texts were translated into rough English prose by Shri Muniji's pupils. I worked that prose into poetic form. Years later this work was published in a collection titled *I Cannot Live Without You*.

Mirabai and Kabir continue to be widely read and celebrated. Kabir was a religious reformer who was initiated by both Hindu and Sufi teachers. Many of his poems are witty, sardonic commentaries on the limitations of his contemporaries' religious attitudes. Mirabai's poetry is very different. Her lyric poems may be divided into intense devotional celebrations of her love for Krishna, which she sang as she danced, and teaching poems that show how to turn devotion into a spiritual practice. Her writing is vividly imagistic and emotionally direct. She likely adopted rhymed couplets from Persian Sufi poets, whose ghazals (devotional lyrics) used that form. So I wrote in rhymed couplets, and also applied what I had learned writing haiku, because Mirabi had a straightforward stance, and her lyric poems requires a direct, unembellished voice.

Six Portraits

Writing haibun stimulated a desire to try writing prose. Prior to travelling to India I experimented with short prose fiction. As just noted, *On Green Dolphin Street* is excerpted from a longer piece written for the abandoned *Portraits of Confusion* project. I intended it to echo the psychological studies of Anais Nin and Jack Kerouac's *The Subterraneans*, but my ability didn't match my ambition. As it now stands, *On Green Dolphin Street* is simultaneously an experiment in William Burrough's cut-up method and a literary jazz improvisation. I followed it by attempting two longer prose pieces, but their style was too florid and didn't work. Accordingly, I returned to the minimalist approach of *Records of a Non-Plussed Being*. However, I needed a Western model. That led me to Ernest Hemingway.

The Travellers is a steal from *Hills Like White Elephants*. It originally had more dialogue, but where Hemingway's dialogue gradually peels back the reason for the couple's tension, my idea lacks that depth. During editing I ended up eliminating all but three words of dialogue, in the process shifting the focus from the couple to the waitress. In *Islands*, written a year later, I kept the observational minimalism but added a more poetic commentary.

The first of the four lyrics was written, like *The Travellers.*, before working on Mirabai's poems. It could be read as providing an emotional backstory to the arguing couple. My brother Ross provided the prompt for attempting song lyrics. He had been playing guitar for a several years and had begun composing songs with Kāren Hunter. They invited me to write lyrics for them. I wrote a handful; they selected and set the first two included here.

In popular music love songs predominate. They usually focus on two or three characters, and they rhyme. Lyrics are also minimalist by nature, so I treated them as exercises in creating portraits in miniature. *The Soldier* is inspired by *The Partisan*, a World War 2 resistance song Leonard Cohen recorded. John Keats' ballad, *La Belle Dame Sans Merci*, lurks in the background. *Old Sal's Tattoo* came from listening to early Beat-inspired Tom Waits.

Mirabai's poems set me up for this. She wrote love lyrics designed to be sung, so in translating her I was already working on lyrics. But another key lesson was involved in lyric writing. Translating Mirabai's poems required me to enter a culture and sensibility very different to my own. I needed to get inside her poems before I could create new versions of them, just as I had to enter the situations depicted in the lyrics in order to write them.

Doing so had far-reaching creative implications. It enabled me to develop a process I utilised in my next two works, *Exile and Return* and *Puck of Starways*. Each involved inhabiting a distinctive character living in a world distant from ours. So a by-product of working on Mirabai's poems and the *Six Portraits* pieces was that it led me to develop a creative process that later flowered in much more complex works: *The Bhagavad Gita*, *The Ecstasy of Cabeza de Vaca* and *Interpretations of Desire*.

Exile and Return

I learned yet another lesson from Mirabai: the power of specificity. Vivid concrete details add emotional power to spiritual writing, which naturally tends towards the abstract. I began to ponder how I could create a sequence of poems, historically grounded, that contained the same passionate directness Mirabai had achieved.

This led me to ancient Jewish wisdom and prophetic literature. I arrived there by way of Saint John of the Cross. I had previously come across the translations of Willis Barstone. I was initially drawn to Saint John's interpretation of Psalm 136 – 'By the waters of Babylon' – and *Spiritual Canticle*, his response to *Song of Songs*.

San Juan transformed the *Song of Songs*' erotic love poetry into an allegorical disquisition on the relationship between the soul as lover and God as the Beloved, which he elucidated in a book-length commentary. From *Spiritual Canticle* I went first to the King James translation of the *Song of Songs*, then began reading the *Psalms*, which expresses a wide range of intense spiritual feelings and thoughts, from ecstatic to despairing. Among the prophetic literature I found *Isaiah* especially appealing. It contains great poetry, with a number of its phrases becoming embedded in the English language via the King James version: man of sorrows, drop in the bucket, like a lamb to the slaughter.

Isaiah is a multi-authored text, written by at least three poet-prophets over a period of one hundred years. In the middle of this period is the exile to Babylon, which began in 597 BCE, when Nebuchadnezzar sacked Jerusalem and deported successive waves of its enslaved inhabitants to Babylon. *Isaiah* echoes the *Psalms* in graphically voicing the religious doubts, intellectual anxieties and emotional pain that overwhelmed the exiles, whose faith in their god Yahweh was understandably tested.

This material attracted me on two levels. Intellectually, Saint John adopted Christian mysticism's three stages of spiritual development, which took me back to my earlier idea of writing a sequence of works structured developmentally. And aesthetically, the Jewish wisdom and prophetic literature centred on the exile to Babylon gave me a historical context, vivid imagery, and, via the King James Bible, a powerful poetic language to work with.

Using these materials, I conceived a sequence of poems consisting of three sections. The first would show the narrator as a slave exiled in Babylon. This is the initial phase of spiritual development, when we begin to appreciate the nature of our emotional and intellectual limitations and seek to escape them. The second section would recount the slave's escape into the wilderness, symbolising a phrase of growth St John of the Cross called the dark night of the soul. This encompasses the individual's struggles during years of inner transformation. The third section would detail a triumphant return to Jerusalem, the exile's home, which symbolises unification of the seeker's various psychospiritual parts. I additionally decided to intersperse through all three parts love poems adapted from the *Song of Songs*, in which the exile addresses his lover, from whom he has long been separated. She represents his deep self, with whom he reconnects during his struggles in the wilderness.

Having worked out this concept, I wrote thirteen poems. I stopped when I realised I didn't know enough to continue. I needed to experience more of what spiritual development involves.

As far as the poetry is concerned, it has many shortcomings. Following Mirabai and the Sufi poets, I employed rhymed couplets. However, many of my rhymes are too obvious. And too often the voice is subservient to the rhythm. After putting the project aside, I returned to it ten years later, reworking the narrative poem by poem, discarding much of what I had originally written. Once I restarted, the sequence took another fourteen years to complete.

Despite the limitations of the poetry in *Exile and Return*, it was a significant exercise. It was my first attempt at adapting existing literary sources, it gave me the confidence to be bolder and broaden the scope of my ideas, and it laid the foundations for *Psalms of Exile and Return*, my most ambitious sequence of poems.

Puck of the Starways

During the 1980s I continued experimenting with fiction. Having already tried short stories, I moved on to writing a novel, then a play. Neither is worth preserving. However, while working on the play a passage spontaneously emerged. Incompatible with the rest, I edited it out. Today it is the only passage worth reading.

Life is old, my friends, and you and I are very young. Long before humankind was even thought of, when the Earth was but a sweating orb of livid seas and violent quaking rock hurtled through the vasts of space, spinning round a yellow sun, certain cosmic laws had long been generating life from vapour and intelligence from life, that the great mystery should not remain deep-hidden, but that managing principles of grand evolvement, and manifesting those principles in actual process, a method and a means might be developed whereby ignorance may grow to know itself.

Thus when the sun embraced the nubile earth, and quick seeds of life espoused the oceans in amoebic form; and when these grew to fish which one day left the muddy shallows to croak and scramble upon the shore; and when from these mammalic firstlings eventually rose a strange and haunted two-legged breed, humankind – for so this new mutation proved to be – was neither unwatched nor unguided. Certain measures had been formed, and all life consequent conformed. It could not do but so. Yet deeper laws also had been drawn, laws which helped evolve not so much the human body as the inner soul and spirit, that the mystery may be turned in upon itself, and human wisdom expanded beyond its sensible limits.

But what do we know of this? For we see only the external form, not the spirit within, and thus the laws pertaining to the deeper mysteries remain concealed – for secrets remain secrets to we who are ourselves secrets, whether knowledge talks of itself, or love herself appears to us. No, we are but primitives standing wide-eyed in the fields of human experience, and until the dawn breaks which will illuminate a path that leads to something other, our days are dull, our nights cold, and both our eyes are filled with darkness. May we not long stand so.

Thematically, this passage reflects my interest in cosmology and evolution and their implications for our spiritual development. This anticipates ideas I explored in much greater detail during the 2010s. Stylistically, the passage is influenced by the language of Shakespeare's late plays. I was drawn to the long rolling sentences, the vivid images and energetic language, the musicality of phrasing. It could be read as a prose poem. As such, this passage wasn't appropriate for a play. But in writing terms it showed a way forward. That way lead to *Puck of the Starways*.

Having failed in my attempts at longer narratives, I decided to return to the short story format. Because my previous prose had been involved with naturalistic stories in a contemporary setting, I decided I would do something completely different and try fantasy. This decision was spurred by my coming across *The Gods of Pegana*, a collection of short stories by Lord Dunsany. I found a 1909 edition of the book while browsing shelves in the Auckland University library.

Fantasy encompasses fairy and folk stories, and particularly tales of the supernatural and its intervention into the everyday. Stories of fairies, knights, dragons, magicians, damsels and crones are sprinkled across all European literatures. Last century this literature influenced the development of romance, horror, science fiction and swords and wizardry, all major sub-genres of fantasy.

Lord Dunsany was at the forefront of last century's turn to fantasy. *The Gods of Pegana*, first published in 1905, describes a pantheon of invented gods and magical beings to whom Dunsany gives outlandish names: Skarl, Limpang-Tung, Mana-Yood-Sushai. The 1909 edition also contains the illustrations of Sidney Sime, who visually matches Dunsany's verbal inventiveness. Each chapter in *The Gods of Pegana* is devoted to a single god or a group of beings. The result is a series of vignettes, rather than developed narratives. Dunsany wrapped it all in a heightened language influenced by the King James Bible.

Having been working with the *Psalms* two months earlier, the idea of using the Bible as a stylistic source for prose had instant appeal. The language of the King James version is robust and rhythmic, and sufficiently flexible to embrace narrative description, lyrical evocation and introspective pondering.

Most of *Puck of the Starways* was written in two months. The idea was to play with and combine various fantasy traditions: religious mythology, fairy stories, folk tales, dreams, and strange and symbolic happenings. While I had read little Jung, I was familiar with his idea of archetypes and the unconscious as a repository of mythological images. These ideas contributed to the work.

One of the most intriguing aspects of fantasy writing is that it involves creating a world which echoes the world we occupy, but contains fantastic variations on it. Of course, the central character is inspired by Shakespeare's Puck and Ariel, with shamanic elements added. As such, *Puck of the Starways* makes explicit an interest that unifies much of my work, of either exploring alternative worlds, fantastical and historical, or examining the 'real' world from an askew perspective. The later interest drove my next project.

Poems of Light and Love

By 1981, as a result of my spiritual exercises, I regularly experienced ecstatic states. For an experiment, I decided to try writing while in such a state. My model was the ghazals of Jalal al-Din Rumi. I had been reading A.J. Arberry's prose translations of Rumi's poems for years, enjoying their ecstatic energy. Rumi's poems are rhymed couplets. Accordingly, I adopted that form. I also felt I had unfinished business with rhymed couplets, given my *Exile and Return* poems were poetically only intermittently successful.

My intention was that these poems would be spontaneous outpourings driven by the energy of an ecstatic state. I adopted two strategies. A number of poems use metaphors drawn from nature combined with tropes of Persian Sufi poetry: spring, birds, sunshine, blossoms, water, wine and drunkenness. My poems in this mode seek to express the exultation of my inner state. The remaining poems are more reflective, and aim to describe my experiences in more straightforward phenomenological terms.

One other influence is at play here. During my final year at university, in a class on American poetry, we looked at *Leaping Poetry*, an essay by Robert Bly. In it Bly argues that poetry needs a quality which he terms dragon smoke. Dragon smoke results when a poem leaps from the known to the unknown and back again. Of course, this is what shamans and mystics do. Bly suggests that Greek and Roman works from the classical era have long leaps at their centres, describing magical events or encounters with gods centred on a leap into the unknown. Bly concludes:

> The real joy of poetry is to experience this leaping inside a poem. A poet who is 'leaping' makes a jump from an object soaked in unconscious psychic substance to an object soaked in conscious psychic substance. ... Thought of in terms of language, leaping is the ability to associate fast.

The poets Bly recalls in support of his idea are Blake, Rimbaud, Lautremont, and the Surrealists, especially the Spanish surrealists, headed by Lorca. These were poets I knew well. Interestingly, Bly also published his own versions of Mirabai's and Kabir's poetry.

I found Bly's theory stimulating. Yet to my mind there was a group of leaping poets he didn't mention: the Persian Sufi poets, including Hafiz, Attar, Jami, Khayyam and Rumi. Sufi practice is precisely to leap between the known and unknown, the physical and the spiritual, the mundane and the supernal. Their poetry is filled with dragon smoke. Even in A.J. Arberry's sober prose translations, it is clear Rumi's ecstatic couplets leap like crazy.

However, writing leaping poetry isn't as straightforward as I had assumed. Couplets are ideal for leaping. They provide options: you can leap from one line to the next inside a couplet, or you can explore one feeling or thought in a couplet, then leap to the next. The big difficulty is the effort required to get the mind leaping. Our mind habitually runs along set tracks, preferring never to go far from its comfort zone. Whenever our mind is jostled out of this zone it quickly settles back into the familiar. Our mind naturally avoids the unfamiliar, the unknown, the scary. It turned out that I needed to write half a dozen poems just to warm up, to shake my mind free of familiar associations and avoid the obvious.

The poems in this sequence were written in two blocks, in 1981 and 1983. Fewer were written in this second period, but they are generally truer to the phenomenology of the moment. Today I consider these poems largely do as intended: not to be utterly out of place when set beside Rumi's ecstatic verses.

Confessions of an Antipodean Mudlark

By 1984 I was feeling I needed to shift gears again. I had written a number of prose pieces, but besides *Puck of the Starways* the only prose worth preserving is the handful of short stories included here, and the satiric *Confessions of An Antipodean Mudlark*.

Looking back, I felt my writing had become too serious. I wanted to loosen up. I had become aware of one way of doing so five years earlier, when Shri Muniji introduced me to Kabir's poetry. Kabir is acerbic in his criticism of the hypocritical ways the Hindus and Muslims of his day practised their religions. Related to this, I had recently read Mark Twain's *Letters from the Earth*, in which he uses Satan writing a report on humanity to cast an acidic eye on us and finding us morally, intellectually and spiritually wanting. The book was so caustic Twain's family feared it would taint his reputation, so forbade its publication until 1962, five decades after his death. Besides Twain's *Letters*, satiric works written in a similar vein that I found impressive were Voltaire's *Candide*, Jonathan Swift's *A Modest Proposal*, and Charles Dicken's 'The Circumlocution Office' chapter in *Little Dorrit*.

Following the lead of Kabir, Swift and Voltaire, I decided to satirise Christianity, and with it the modern world. By now I had become aware of how Christian missionaries facilitated European powers colonising native populations in order to exploit their land's natural resources. I used the colonialisation of New Zealand to ground the pieces. I also returned to Alfred Jarry for inspiration. In his *Exploits & Opinions of Dr. Faustroll, Pataphysician*, Jarry proposes a new science that extends as far beyond metaphysics as metaphysics extends beyond physics:

> Pataphysics will examine the laws governing exceptions, and will explain the universe supplementary to this one; or, less ambitiously, will describe a universe which can be – and perhaps should be – envisaged in the place of the traditional one.

Jarry satirises science not from disdain, but because he found its advances so fascinating – he wrote *Faustroll* just a few years before Einstein published his theory of relativity. I decided to adopt Jarry's approach in relation to religion. Hence I created the philosophy of matterphysics: its querulous attitude drives *Confessions*.

From a craft perspective, these essays offered a new challenge. They combine precise intellectual argument, ludicrous invention, symbolic language, allegorical (mis)interpretation, piss-take logic and ironic social commentary. These essays became exercises in maintaining consistency of tone, language and thought. They added to the two one act plays as sardonic works I wrote in 1984.

Jerusalem, 52 CE

Between 1986 and 1989 I undertook my largest writing project to date: a full-length play, *The Gnosis of Simon Magus*. Simon Magus is popularly known as a charlatan and heretic. However, historical records suggest a more complex, and more interesting, character. Simon's Christian enemies wrote he was a pupil of John the Baptist. After the Baptist's death, Simon went to Alexandria. His later denigrators claimed he studied magic there.

Intriguingly, Alexandria was also a major centre for the esoteric schools of Neoplationism, Hermeticism and Gnosticism. While Gnosticism is historically considered to be a Christian heresy, many Gnostics were not Christians at all, rather being aligned with Greco-Egyptian, Judaic, Greek or Mesopotamian traditions. Writings ascribed to Simon Magus (including his appellation of Magus) suggest he drew on Zoroastrian teachings, and was influenced, as many thinkers then were, by Neoplatonic thought.

The first and second centuries were a period of extraordinary spiritual vitality. Besides the many Gnostic groups, the Essenes, Therapeuts, Nazoreans and Mandeans each had significant communities, while rabbinic schools were reading the *Song of Songs* mystically and writing the texts that laid the foundations for the Kabbalah. This period also featured struggles between Christian communities as they sought to establish themselves doctrinally and socially. *The Gnosis of Simon Magus* is set in Jerusalem in 52 CE, when the political situation was as fraught as the religious one.

Originally, Paul of Tarsus was one of the play's central characters. However, I decided the play was too long, so edited him out. The speeches included here are among those I excised. When deciding on a language to use for *Simon Magus*, I initially tried the language of the one act plays. However, it wasn't rich enough. After experimenting, I selected blank verse as the most appropriate. It is flexible, enabling shifts in tone between intense emotion, political speechifying and arcane philosophising.

Paul is complex. He persecuted Christians on behalf of the Jewish authorities until his 'road to Damascus' experience converted him to Christianity. After joining those he had been repressing, he helped shape the early Christian revelation. The doctrines he taught included the significance of the resurrection, the concepts that define being Christian, and the evils of schismatic teachings. That many contending doctrines were circulating among Christians during the first century is evidenced in his letters:

> It is clear there are serious differences among you. What I mean are all these slogans that you have, like 'I am for Paul', 'I am for Apollos', 'I am for Cephas', 'I am for Christ'. (1 Corinthians 1 11-12) ... Let me warn you that if anyone preaches a version of the Good News different from the one we have already preached to you, whether it be ourselves or an angel from heaven, he is to be condemned. (Galatians 1 6-8)

Paul didn't just condemn wayward Christians. Other letters suggest he was vehemently anti-Gnostic. That Paul was anti-Gnostic remained a given until an extensive cache of Gnostic writings was discovered in Nag Hammadi, Egypt, in 1945. They show that early Christianity was more complicated, and nuanced, than official history allows. Notably, the documents show that Christian Gnostic groups, who should have rejected Paul after being condemned by him, in fact revered him as a great teacher. Valentinius, a leading Egyptian Gnostic, claimed to have been taught by Theudas, who was a pupil of Paul. Theodotus, another influential Gnostic teacher, maintained that Paul taught on two levels, tailoring his teachings for beginners (called psychics) and the advanced (the elect):

> On the one hand he preached the saviour 'according to the flesh' as one 'who was born and suffered', the kerygmatic gospel of 'Christ crucified' (1 Corinthians 2:2) to those who were psychics, 'because of this they were

capable of knowing, and in this way they feared him.' But to the elect he proclaimed Christ 'according to the spirit, as one born from spirit and a virgin' (Romans 1:3) for the apostle recognised that 'each one knows the Lord in his own way: and not all know him alike.'

I responded to this perspective by writing speeches that combine materials from the *Acts*, Paul's letters, and Gnostic treatises and prayers, to reveal Paul's Gnostic affiliation. In his letters Paul distinguished between actions performed according to religious law and those inspired by direct personal revelation, gnosis. Religious law is performed by beginners, who Paul addressed in public, while gnosis is experienced by the advanced, taught by Paul privately.

Paul's final address presents ideas ascribed to him by later Gnostics. This suggests another path Western spirituality might have followed, a more open-minded, less coercive path, driven by individual insight rather than by doctrines imposed top-down. Individual discovery is an option Christianity, and so Western culture, rejected. That rejection was itself widely rejected last century, when the dissatisfied turned to non-Christian spiritual concepts and practices.

The Fall and The Saviour

After spending three years researching, writing and rewriting *Simon Magus*, I felt I wasn't yet done with theatre. In part that was because I knew *Simon Magus* would be so expensive to mount, and its topic is so distant from modern concerns, it is unlikely to ever be performed.

Additionally, I felt the themes I had explored in my first two one act plays hadn't been fully plumbed. Today, of course, the foundational myths of Christianity are no longer central to our culture. Grotowski writes about how old myths lose their hold, how we embrace new myths, and the ways theatre may contribute to this process:

The theatre, when it was still part of religion, was already theatre: it liberated the spiritual energy of the congregation or tribe by incorporating myth and profaning or rather transgressing it. The spectator thus had a renewed awareness of his personal truth in the truth of the myth, and through fright and a sense of the sacred he came to catharsis. ... But today's situation is much different. As social groupings are less and less defined by religion, traditional mythic forms are in flux, disappearing and being reincarnated.

The greatest of the Greek tragedians, Aeschylus, Sophocles and Euripides, dramatised the myths of their era, stretching them, testing their implications. On one occasion, Aeschylus had to run from angry audience members who mistakenly thought he had publicly revealed the sacrosanct mysteries. In several plays Euripides criticises the Greeks' self-destructive addiction to warring, which they justified by mythologising their heroic place in the world. In *The Bacchae* he dramatises the myth of Dionysius to explore the excesses of ecstatic freeing revelation and repressive law, a juxtaposition of stances that continues to be relevant today, given we have zealots of various economic, political and religious creeds striving to impose on the rest of us their view of how the world should be. The author of the *Wakefield Pageants* similarly played with Christian narratives, re-imagining Biblical characters as contemporary English workers to show that the myths supporting the Christian revelation remained relevant in late medieval England. These writers could treat myths this way because they and their audiences shared the same mythologies, and so appreciated what the drama was exploring, extrapolating, interrogating, challenging.

But what happens when, as Grotowksi notes, 'traditional mythic forms are in flux'? How can we profane, transgress or transform ancient myths that no longer resonate with us, and so no longer engage us at a deep level?

In practice, the most influential myths do not disappear. As Grotowski observes, they reincarnate and, transmogrified into new forms, continue to haunt humanity's psychic cellars, where culturally shaped assumptions lurk long after the demise of their originating impulse. The Greek and Roman practice of creating myths to uphold their heroic place in the world was adopted by nineteenth century European nations as they colonised peoples they viewed as culturally, religiously, racially, morally and intellectually inferior. Today, aggressive countries invade others' lands, and assault portions of their own populations, physically, politically, economically, culturally and psychologically, using similar self-heroising myths to justify their actions.

The myth of the apocalypse, promoted by Zarathustra around 1200 BCE, remains alive for billions, to the extent that many enthusiasts are attempting to bring it about in the Middle East, where followers of the Abrahamic religions assume it will occur. This myth is also alive in non-religious contexts, particularly in speculations regarding our environmental, technological and political trajectories. That we have so many dystopian narratives of the future that focus on various kinds of prohibition and destruction, and very few positive portraits of what we could become, indicates the (death?) grip the myth of the apocalypse has on the modern psyche.

The myth of a God-backed elite dates to, and likely precedes, the rise of the first Bronze Age cities in Mesopotamia, Egypt and India during the fourth millennia BCE. Socially, they divided their populaces into three strata: a God-annointed king, a ruling class of aristocrats and priests, and commoners, whose labour drove the state economically. Below everyone were slaves. Those ancient social divisions remain in place today. Populaces are divided into the classes of rulers, elites and commoners according to hereditary, wealth and status. Work and sex slaves and child labourers support everyone above them. Many endorse this myth, justifying it with appeals to God, blood, historical privilege, genetic superiority, racial inferiority, cultural difference and psychophysical incapacity. Having now been embedded in human social relations for well over five thousand years, the myth of the superior elite is so enthusiastically embraced by the exploited majority it will not vanish any time soon.

The myth of the saviour who will liberate the world is one of our most pernicious. The New Testament attests the first Christians expected Jesus would return to Earth within a generation. Two thousand years later they are still waiting. But they don't wait alone. Hope-filled Buddhist, Judaic and Islamic believers anticipate the arrival of their own saviours. And today's non-religious masses equally fervently hope for a saviour in the form of a politician, technology genius, billionaire or celebrity, who will – any day now – step up to liberate us all from the worst of what we have brought about. The weakness of the myth of the saviour is that it puts the onus on someone else to make the big decisions. The current state of the planet evidences the fallacy of this myth. Thinking about this led me to the themes I explore in *The Fall* and *The Saviour*: coercion, expectation, passivity, taking responsibility.

Before writing these plays I had come across Peter Brook's demarcation of theatre into the categories of holy, rough and contemporary, and been struck by his observation that the strongest theatre combines all three. According to Brook's schemata, *Simon Magus* is holy theatre that lacks rough and contemporary aspects. I decided my next plays would add these elements.

Thinking about rough theatre took me back to Jarry's *Ubu Roi*. Jarry gave the actors masks and had them use exaggerated puppet gestures, much like Punch and Judy. Early last century Edward Gordon Craig and Vsevolod Meyerhold toyed with using puppets instead of actors in their productions. Like Jarry, they were responding to the ways rapidly expanding industrialism was diminishing people's collective humanity.

The Fall adopts this puppet concept literally, requiring the actors to perform as string puppets, with the unseen puppet master echoing Beckett's ploy of the on-stage action being driven by a manipulating off-stage presence. *The Saviour* was conceived to contrast with *The Fall*.

It draws on a combination of gesture, repetition, non sequiturs and slapstick to critique the myth of the saviour.

Thematically, the four plays that constitute *A Brief History of the World* play with myths that have shaped the Western religious metaphysic. In thematic order: *The Fall* deals with the mythological era, when humanity was dependent on the gods in all phases of life; *The Saviour* depicts the era of saviour gods, in which humanity became more political and self-involved, with religion centred on a personal relationship with a God who will save human beings one by one; *The Catalogue of an Ordinary Life* is set in the present era, in which humanity's outlook is essentially materialistic and conditioned by the concept of personal rewards and punishments, with religion reduced to a social construct; and *Innerworld of the Underworld* deals with humanity's primal dilemma of seeking to evolve spiritually on this planet, while quagmired in the overwhelmingly negative forces we have put into play. This is not necessarily the order in which they may best be performed.

Collaboration with Dawn Tuffery has resulted in *The Fall* and *Innerworld of the Underworld* being made into animated films. Inspired by Jarry's puppet concept, and Brooks' notion of rough theatre, the two films rework the original texts, recontextualising their settings and narratives so they work as animations.

Conclusion

The work collected here was written as the twentieth century was bringing about a series of endings: the end of colonialism, the end of communism, the end of metaphysics. A view was even canvassed that the high civilisation of the secular, liberal, capitalist West had brought about the end of history, that life in the 1980s West was as good as human existence could get. The arts reflected the intellectual zeitgeist by proclaiming the end of modernism, the collapse of grand narratives, the fall of the canon, the demise of the novel, the death of the author, even the end of the book.

So, after all those endings, where have we got to? What is coming next? But, of course, nothing that significantly impacts our lives actually ends. World War One, declared the War to End All Wars, was soon followed by World War Two. Postmodern, feminist, post-colonial and ecological critiques of power, institutions, hierarchy, patriarchy and social injustice have not ended them. People deflect. Institutions recalibrate. The world goes on. Yet the question remains: On to what? After viewing Mondrian's paintings, New Zealand artist Colin McCahon addressed this question by stating:

> Mondrian, it seemed to me, came up in this century as a great barrier – the painting to END all painting. As a painter, how do you get around either a Michelangelo or a Mondrian? It seems that the only way is not more 'masking tape' but more involvement in the human situation.

When faced with a blockage, with an apparent ending, human beings inevitably use their creativity to find another way to move forwards. McCahon reminds us that evolving creatively is not a matter of doing more of what we have always done, in the way we always have done it. Rather, it involves changing our trajectory. For McCahon, the solution to the problem of creating new painting was not to be found in the plastics of painting or in the activity of being a painter, but in exploring our shared human situation.

Ultimately, we value art because we use it to tell each other what it is to be human. No single artwork encapsulates everything that may be said. Each embodies just an aspect of our multi-faceted existence. Art, at its most profound, expresses our desire to understand what, why and how the world is as it is. And we are as we are. We necessarily each do this in our own way, according to our personal inner drives, within the opportunities provided by our life circumstances, given the kinds of experiences we have had, and with the means each of us has at our disposal. Ultimately, this is why artists create art, scientists research, theologians generate God-talk, thinkers analyse and prophesy, and writers churn out words.

Looking back, the journey I have undertaken is not one it would occur to many writers to embark on. In fact, it didn't occur to me. I just engaged with what I found attractive. That attraction has sustained an exploration that has taken me into many different literatures, and drawn me to the rapturous and illuminating texts that I found inspiring. I hope the resulting work is as stimulating to read as it has been to write. If not, then to repeat the apt words of William Blake: 'Forgive what you do not approve, and love me for this energetic exertion of my talent.'

References

p 15   'Know what is in your sight ...' A. Guillaumont., Henri-Charles
        Puech, Gilles Quispel, Walter Till, Yassah Abd Al Masih,
        translators, *The Gospel According to Thomas* (Harper and Row,
        1959), logia 5, p 5.

p 181   'Blessed is the lion ...' Ibid, logia 7, p 5.

p 157   'I am now trying an experiment ...' from Jonathan Swift, *Tale
        of the Tub.*

p 161   All Bible quotations are from *The Jerusalem Bible* (Darton,
        Longman & Todd, 1966).

p 209   'Why are we concerned with art? ...' Jerzy Grotowski, *Towards
        a Poor Theatre* (Simon and Schuster, 1968), pp 21-22.

p 213   'In hell for to dwell ...' Anonymous, *Everyman*, A.C. Crawley,
        editor (Manchester University Press, 1961), line 79, p 3.

p 215   'The word cruelty ...' Antonin Artaud, *The Theatre and Its
        Double* (Calder and Boyers, 1970), pp 79-80.

p 218   'to express objectively secret truths ...' Ibid, p 51.

p 220   'The Creator from the spreading of fervour ...' Idries Shah,
        The Sufis (Jonathan Cape, 1969), p 113.

p 220   'the ravings of a madman', ibid.

p 221   'menacing machine', from the poem *Terror Conduction*, Philip
        Lamantia, *Bed of Spinxes: New & Selected Poems 1943-1993* (City
        Lights Books, 1997), p 29.

p 222   'I am following her ...' Ibid, p 22.

p 235   'The real joy of poetry ...' Robert Bly, *Leaping Poetry: An Idea
        with Poems and Translations* (Beacon Press, 1975), p 4.

p 237   'Pataphysics will examine the laws ...' Alfred Jarry, *Exploits &
        Opinions of Dr. Faustroll, Pataphysician*, Simon Watson Taylor,
        translator (Exact Exchange, 1996), p 22.

p 239   'On the one hand he preached ...' Elaine Pagels, *The Gnostic
        Paul: Gnostic Exegesis of the Pauline Letters* (Fortress Press,
        1975), p 5.

p 241   'The theatre, when it was still ...' Grotowski, pp 22-23.

p 245   'Mondrian, it seems to me ...' Colin McCahon, *Colin McCahon: A survey exhibition* (Auckland City Art Gallery, 1972), p 28.

p 246   'Forgive what you do not approve ...' 'Jerusalem', *Blake: Complete Writings*, Geoffrey Keynes, editor (Oxford University Press, 1974), p 621.

Other books referenced

Anonymous, *The Wakefield Pageants in the Towneley Cycle*. A.C. Crawley, editor, Manchester University Press, 1958.

Karen Armstrong. *A History of God*. Vintage, 1999.

Matsuo Bashō. *The Narrow Road to the Deep North and Other Travel Sketches*. Nobuyuki Yuasa, translator, Penguin, 1967.

Peter Brook. *The Empty Space*. Penguin, 1968.

Issa. *The Year of My Life: A Translation of Issa's Oraga Haru*. Nobuyuki Yuasa, translator, University of California Press, 1973.

Alfred Jarry. *Selected Works of Alfred Jarry*. Simon Watson Taylor, translator, Grove Press, 1965.

St John of the Cross. *The Poems of St. John of the Cross*. Willis Barnstone, translator. New Directions, 1972.

Peter Jones. *Imagist Poetry*. Penguin, 1972.

Ferderico Garcia Lorca. *The Selected Poems of Federico Garcia Lorca*. F. G. Lorca and Donald M. Allen, editors, New Directions, 1961.

G.R.S. Mead. *Simon Magus*. Ares Publishers, reprint of 1896 edition.

James M. Robinson, general editor. *The Nag Hammadi Library In English*. Harper and Row, 1981.

Jalal al-Din Rumi. *Mystical Poems of Rumi*. A.J. Arberry, translator, The University of Chicago Press, 1974.

Mark Twain. *Letters from the Earth: Uncensored Writings by Mark Twain*. Bernardo DeVoto, editor. Harper and Row, 1962.

Acknowledgements

We live in an extraordinary period. Vast tracts of contemporary and historical knowledge are available to anyone who wishes to explore them. This means that although I live in New Zealand, and am no specialist, I have been able to access literary, cultural and mystical texts from multiple cultures and eras. This access is extensive in its scale and detail, but exists only as a result of the work of countless historians, philologists, translators and scholars. Their work has enabled me to draw from extensive reservoirs of human experience, thought and insight. Without others having dedicated their lives to these arcane areas of human history, my cross-cultural, multi-era exploration would never have been possible. For their work I am utterly grateful.

Through the years I have been inspired by generous teachers. Alan Trussell-Cullen introduced me to poetry when I was aged nine. Trevor Dobbin introduced me to Shakespeare, became a valued friend, and over the years offered many appreciated comments on my writing. At Auckland University all lecturers balanced knowledge with passion, but several stood out to me personally: Jack Marshall for William Blake, Sydney Musgrove for Shakespeare, Roger Horrocks for American poetry and film, Sebastian Black for twentieth century drama and fiction, Leonard bell for art history, and Clive Pearson for metaphysics and pre-Socratic philosophy.

I add grateful thanks to my spiritual teachers, Abdullah Dougan and Shri Muniji Maharaj. Thanks also to two writers: Peggy Dunstan for her poetry group, where I learned how to critique my work, and Alistair Paterson, who published some early poems and offered astute feedback. At Auckland University Murray Lynch workshopped *The Catalogue of an Ordinary Life*, which showed me my concept for theatre could work. Finally, my gratitude to Gregory Richards for introducing me to art and literature created far beyond New Zealand's shores.

To the reader

Small presses rely on the support of readers to tell others about the books they enjoy. To support this book and its author, we ask you to consider placing a review on the site where you bought it. Other books by Keith Hill related to this collection may be viewed on www.attarbooks.com and are available from all online bookstores:

The God Revolution

Winner Best Book Ashton Wylie Book Awards 2011

Hill's exposition is a fine example of scrupulously rigorous scholarship – it is remarkable how much ground is covered within his brief historical survey. In addition, he discusses a wide range of academically abstruse subjects in consistently lucid, nontechnical prose. ... An impressive and accessible intro-duction to a challenging philosophical topic. – Kirkus Review

A writer in the vein of Karen Armstrong – a rationalist whose research has led to obvious but ground-breaking conclusions. The Ashton Wylie Chari-table Trust Book Award, which celebrates New Zealand's forward thinkers, is thoroughly deserved. – Mike Alexander, *Sunday Star Times*

Books of this calibre, written and published here in New Zealand, are a rare phenomena. This deserves to be read by all those who care about ideas, the trajectory of civilization and its future form. – Peter Dornauf

Over the past four hundred years social, scientific and intellectual revolutions have radically altered our understanding of reality. At the same time a diverse range of thinkers have developed equally radical ideas about God. *The God Revolution* examines the complex historical and cultural reasons the Western idea of a personal God came under siege, culminating in Nietzsche's declaration, 'God is dead'. It explores the ideas of key thinkers who treated Nietzsche's proclamation as a challenge and developed intriguing new ideas about God and reality. It concludes with a summary of the current state of new thinking about God.

The Ecstasy of Cabeza de Vaca

A tour de force. A truly original and remarkable recasting in verse of the ill-fated Narváez expedition to Central America. Hill's humanizing of de Vaca is the ingredient that makes it so moving and once taken up, impossible to put down. – Alistair Paterson

In a series of extraordinary encounters depicted in beautifully rendered action and imagery. Hill makes de Vaca's inner world spring to wondrous life. Natural, memorable and rewarding. – Raewyn Alexander

An extraordinary effort of imagination. In New Zealand literature there's certainly no long poem like this one. – Roger Horrocks

In 1528, a Spanish expedition was shipwrecked in the Gulf of Mexico. Eight years later only four men remained alive. One of the four, Cabeza de Vaca, later published an account of what occurred. Naked and enslaved, de Vaca was stripped of all he possessed, then underwent an extraordinary transformation. *The Ecstasy of Cabeza de Vaca* is Keith Hill's masterful retelling of Cabeza de Vaca's story. This is a heartbreaking account of courage and faith, barbarity and miracles, that transports us to the limits of human experience.

Puck of the Starways

Beautifully written, draws in the reader. – Alyson Walton
A masterpiece. – John Psathas

'Day in and day out, never resting, Puck played. Having no body, he flitted from star to star, solar system to solar system. Ever at fun, he gambolled through the ten thousand veils of reality. Life to him was a joy, and that joy was his life's whole meaning ... '

So begin the adventures of Puck. In a series of linked stories, Puck delights in the wonders, comedies, sorrows and joys that enrich human existence. Spinning tales that delight and confound, playfully mixing magic with metaphysics, the fabulous with moral questions, this is an inspired addition to fantasy story-telling in the tradition of Lord Dunsay, Alberto Calvino and Ursula Le Guin.

Psalms of Exile and Return

In a time that seems spiritually dry for so many, this book of psalms is water in the desert. They challenge, terrify, comfort, and call us to a deep humanity. – Allan Jones, Dean Emeritus, Grace Cathedral, San Francisco

In 587 BCE, King Zedekiah of Judah led his people in rebellion against Babylonian rule. Nebuchadnezzar responded mercilessly. His army sacked Jerusalem, destroyed the Temple, and deported thousands to Babylon. These psalms are written from the perspective of one of those exiles. They express his growing unhappiness with life as a slave, his despairing cries for help to his Lord, and his eventual escape into the wilderness. After much struggle he is reunited with his lost beloved, and together they reach Jerusalem.

Inspired by the impassioned Jewish prophets and poets, and in harmony with the Jewish healing tradition of tikkun olam, these poems recount seekers' spiritual journey as they strive to transcend everyday life, enter their own hurt heart, heal its pain, and release the wisdom that exists there. It is the story of exiles who, lost and despairing, rediscover themselves in joy.

Interpretations of Desire

Mystical love poems by the Sufi Master Ibn 'Arabi

Keith Hill's artful and beautiful renditions will bring Ibn 'Arabi's neglected masterpiece to a new readership. – Nile Green, *Sufism: A Global History*

In 1201, Shaykh Muhyiddin Ibn 'Arabi arrived in Mecca. Among those who impressed him was Nizám, the daughter of a prominent religious teacher. As Beatrice did for Dante, Nizám soon inspired a sequence of love poems that are Ibn 'Arabi's poetic masterpiece, *Tarjumán al-Aswáq* (*The Interpreter of Desire*).

Ibn 'Arabi was known as Shaykh al-Akbar (the Greatest Shaykh), a title given him due to his profound knowledge as a mystic, theologian, philosopher and legalist. However, while scholars are translating his key prose words into English, his poetry remains little known. This collection reveals that with his intense feeling, vivid imagery, and the playful way he reworked the conventions of Bedouin desert poetry, Ibn 'Arabi wrote poems that deserve to be placed alongside the best of his fellow Sufi poets, including Rumi, Attar, Jami and Hafiz.

I Cannot Live Without You
Selected Poems of Mirabai and Kabir

It's been an eternity since I was hungry for God's pure essence. I Cannot Live Without You *reignites a deep passion to see the face of God, even knowing that God has no face. This book will renew your hunger for your sacred flame.*
– Judith Hoch PhD, *Prophecy on the River*

Wild and passionate, Mirabai is India's greatest poet of devotion and love. Married at a young age, after her husband's premature death she dedicated her life to worshipping the flute-playing Krishna. It was a decision that led her parents-in-law to evict her from their home. Mirabai spent the rest of her life travelling from village to village, singing and dancing to celebrate her love of Krishna. The rapturous lyrics she wrote enthralled worshippers then and continue to be sung in India today.

Kabir was a controversial figure. An illiterate weaver, he celebrated both Indian and Muslim spirituality, while criticising each religion's blinkered believers. Yet his straight talking, his wit, and the continued relevance of his insights, ensure his often knotty poems still resonate powerfully with contemporary readers.

The Bhagavad Gita
A new poetic translation

On the battlefield of life, desiring to do our best, how should we act? Which values should we live by? What metaphysical outlook best explains what happens to us? How do we express our spiritual nature? And how can we stay spiritually focused in the whirl of daily activity?

Arjuna's searching questions, asked on the brink of a war he is loathe to fight, and Krishna's profound answers, spoken in his chariot as they survey the battlefield on which thousands will soon die, offer timeless insights into the difficulties and wonders of human existence, making the *Bhagavad Gita* one of the great works of world spirituality.

Originally written in poetry, but commonly translated into English in prose, this version balances the need to present the *Bhagavad Gita's* profound concepts precisely while reproducing the original's dramatic and poetic power. This translation is especially successful in capturing the *Bhagavad Gita's* shifts of tone, moving from vivid descriptions of the battlefield, to the precise reasoning of Krishna's advice to Arjuna, to the sublime visionary intensity of Krishna as cosmic being. Endnotes and a glossary help readers unfamiliar with Indian culture understand the poem's mythological and philosophic references.

Out of the Way World Here Comes Humanity!

Top 10 Poetry Book for 2022, NZ Listener

'A satirist in the tradition of Juvenal and Swift. Hill shoots his barbs in many directions. Irony, really heavy irony, is Hill's most constant weapon. Addressing the problem of species becoming extinct, his poem *We Need to Stop Dithering* suggests we put these animals out of their misery by eating them and maybe storing their DNA for future use. You may guess what tone he strikes in dealing with imperfect democracy, Donald Trump, climate change, workers' rights and the unequal distribution of wealth.

What did I eventually feel after reading this melange of anger, irony, accusation and Juvenalian satire? Frankly elated. Okay, it's raucous and ranty in places, but this collection is hard to put down. A great holiday from more polite and cryptic poetry.'
– Nicholas Reid, NZ *Listener*

The Gnosis of Simon Magus

Simon Magus is an enigma. Long derided as a heretic magician, the first enemy of Christianity, the truth is much more complex.

And fascinating. This dramatic retelling of Simon's story draws on documentary and legendary materials that show him to be a misunderstood pioneer of Western spirituality. An in-depth background essay explores his connection to Gnostic thought and how he came to be declared an enemy of Christianity.

The Gnosis of Simon Magus is an imaginative retelling of Simon's story. It is set in Jerusalem in 52 CE, a city occupied by Rome. A puppet king sits in the palace, the populace is seething, and the Roman army's presence is provoking rebellion rather than instilling peace. In this cauldron, Jesus' apostle Kepa is struggling to guide the first Christian community.

Enter Simon Magus. After the death of John the Baptist, Simon travelled to Egypt to study spiritual philosophy and penetrate the mysteries of magic. Twenty years after Jesus' crucifixion, he returns to Jerusalem with a former prostitute who knew Jesus well and lights another fuse in a city ready to explode.

Striving To Be Human

How can we act morally in the modern world?

Winner Best Unpublished Manuscript Ashton Wylie Book Awards 2006

It is often difficult differentiating between what's genuinely right for everyone and what just feels right to do.

Over the last century the human world has become a complex arena filled with competing viewpoints. Traditional religious strictures have been replaced with secular laws, ethics have shifted from God-fearing and restrictive to liberal and relativist, and multiculturalism has revealed the extent to which values are socially constructed. Yet rather than now feeling liberated from the mores of the past, many are bewildered. Seeking a solid moral centre for their life, they advocate for values drawn from familiar religious, political, cultural, scientific or business creeds.

In *Striving To Be Human*, Keith Hill evaluates this situation by seeking a moral yardstick that is relevant in today's secular, multicultural world. Using non-technical language, and drawing on the work of leading thinkers, cultural innovators and spiritual pioneers from a wide range of disciplines and eras, he considers how traditional religious values fell out of sync with the modern world view and weighs the new perspectives proposed to replace them.

Striving To Be Human provides valuable insights for those who wish to understand how modern moral attitudes have developed and who seek to identify which values remain relevant in today's complex world.

For more on Keith Hill's books go to www.keithhillauthor.com. Sample passages may be viewed on www.attarbooks.com.

Milton Keynes UK
Ingram Content Group UK Ltd.
UKHW011437140724
445326UK00004B/275